FROM THE WRECKAGE

Michele G. Miller

Titles by Author

Visit my website for updates: www.michelegmillerbooks.coM

This book is dedicated to T-Town
(Tuscaloosa, Alabama), Joplin, Missouri
and all those who have suffered from the
wrath of Mother Nature. The human spirit
will always endure

"Take away love, and our earth is a tomb" -Robert Browning

One

"Is this on?"

Jules' eyes flick to the small television across the room as she takes her place in the faded velvet wingback chair. Her own face stares back at her from the screen, indicating the camera is indeed working. Out of habit, her hands run over her strawberry blonde hair. She twirls a curl around her finger and brushes her long bangs to the side. Satisfied with her appearance, she takes a deep breath.

"Okay, Hi," her hand lifts in a small wave. "I'm Jules Blacklin from Tyler, Texas. Oh, crap. No, I shouldn't wave."

Shimmying backward, she works to find a comfortable sitting position; her sundress catching against the velvet nap of the seat cushion. With a low sigh, she runs her hand between her skirt and the chair. Freeing the fabric, Jules adjusts the dress again and crosses her legs daintily, while stealing another glance at the television screen, checking her appearance.

She'd set up the small twenty-inch screen on a side table so she could see herself as a video camera recorded her story. Although now the camera makes her more uneasy. Sitting here, watching herself speak to nobody makes her question her sanity. It feels like something a crazy person would do.

With a thoughtful eye, she watches herself lean forward and rest her elbow on the armrest. She goes with the pose; it makes her look studious.

"Okay, yeah. . . That's good," she speaks aloud.

With a demure nod of her head, she begins again.

"Hi. My name is Jules Blacklin, Hillsdale High class of 2014. I'm making this video essay as my contribution to the class of 2014, time capsule. I . . ."

She pauses, her mind blanking out for a spell as she smiles into the lens recording her. She takes a moment, steadying her thoughts before continuing. "I want to tell you about myself. About what I've been through, and what the town of Tyler has been through. Winston Churchill once said, 'Sure I am of this, that you have only to endure to conquer.' Rest assured—I have endured. I have endured, and now I am ready to conquer."

Jules gives herself a mental high-five for remembering the quote and releases a deep breath. With her hands clasped, she leans forward in her seat. Her blue eyes stare directly into the red blinking light indicating the camera is recording.

"I'm inviting you on a journey. A journey through my senior year. Actually, if you're watching this, I'm going to ask you to be a bystander. See, I'm not making this for you. I'm recording this for the ones who didn't live, the ones I will forever be mindful of. For the ones I knew, the ones I didn't . . . and especially for the ones I loved. This is for you."

Uncrossing her legs, she leans back in the chair again; her eyes continuing to connect with the nameless faces that will someday watch this DVD. She settles back for her long story, her finger tracing the scrolling pattern across her skirt. She gathers herself, her thoughts and memories. It's a few moments—a flash of time—but for her, in her mind she sees everything. Once more, her pale gaze meets the lens and she decides where to start.

"Let's begin with your ending. The last night my life was normal. The last night we were *all* normal."

Two

Her eyes close and she allows her mind to wander back to that muggy Friday night. The late August Texas heat is so thick you can cut through it. In her mind, she can still hear the crowd cheering at the first football game of the season. She recalls the buzzing of the Friday night lights illuminating the football field on campus. The smashing of helmets blend in with the constant, exuberant play-by-play calls of Nick 'Voice of the Mustangs' Swanson in the background.

Her chest tightens at the perfect memories, and she fast forwards to the parking lot after the game. As if reading a story, she describes the night, the conversations, the feelings . . .

"Hey Jules?" Stuart's low voice murmurs into her neck as his warm lips make their way up her throat. Her skin leaps at the touch of his fingers as they skim the skin at the base of her cheerleading uniform top.

"Hmmm?"

"I love seeing you back in this little outfit again." He chuckles and slips his fingers under her top and up her spine.

She laughs lightly. "Mmm hmmm, of course you do."

The gym door slams open behind them, and Jules gently pushes Stuart away. They're leaning against his car in the student parking lot after the first football game of the season. The Hillsdale Mustangs easily handled their rival team, the Rossview Knights, with a score of twenty-four to three. Now they're waiting for the rest of their friends so they can head out and celebrate. It's the last weekend of summer break—come Monday morning, school will be back in session.

"Hey lovebirds, you ready?"

Jules glances over Stuart's shoulder as he leans into her once more and gives her best friend a quick nod of acknowledgment. Tanya smirks and heads toward her car.

The metal door flies open once more ricocheting off the brick wall of the school building as guys from the football team pour out; their laughing and trash-talking fills the air.

"Let's go back to my place. My parents won't be back until tomorrow." Stuart presses a soft kiss by her ear, ignoring the commotion around them.

"Stop," she whispers, all the while wrapping her hands around his back and holding him closer.

"C'mon, doll. We can celebrate alone for a change."

"Hey, Stu!"

His face close to Jules' neck, Stuart sighs at the interruption, responding with a loud, somewhat annoyed, "What?"

"Coach was looking for you. He had something he wanted to run by you, I think."

Lifting his arm, he lets his teammate know he heard him, and turns his attention back to Jules; touching his forehead to hers. Even with his face partially shadowed by the street lights, she can make out his puppy dog pout.

"Whatcha say? Just me and you tonight?"

Jules doesn't waver. Trying to soften the suggestion he won't like, she presses a small kiss to his lips. "Let's go to the Shack, okay?"

"I'm so tired of Friday nights at the Shack, Jules. Man! I can't wait to get to USC and have more to do." Obviously angry, he steps back and slides next to her; propping his tall, lean frame against the car door.

"Um, okay. Sorry you're so tired of us here in Texas, surfer boy," she grumbles; facing him and giving his foot a playful kick with the toe of her tennis shoe.

A slight grin teases Stuart's lips. "Aren't you, though? Aren't you ready to get out of here too?"

"We've had this conversation a million times. I'm staying in Texas. I love it here. It's my home."

"I know."

She's grateful when the sharp blast of a car horn interrupts their conversation. They both look up as Tanya's stops in front of them, her other best friend Katie riding shotgun in the passenger seat. "We're heading out. Y'all gonna stay here all night or are you coming?"

Jules opens her mouth to send them on their way, but Stuart beats her to the punch. "She's riding with you two," he shouts, pushing away from the car.

"I'm what?" She can't believe he's seriously not coming with her. They've been dating for almost two years now, Friday nights at the Shack are a way of life in Tyler. Especially for the football team.

"Ride with them and I'll meet you. I need to go see Coach, remember?" he reminds her, leaning in for another long kiss.

"Get a room," her best friends heckle from the car as they break into obnoxious giggles and crank up a Taylor Swift song.

Jules laughs against Stuart's mouth as Tanya and Katie shout about being 'Twenty-two.' Their voices resemble cats in heat and she cringes, laughing hard the longer they go on.

Stuart growls at the loss of her lips and drops his forehead against her shoulder. She pats the top of his silky blond head, consoling him.

"Damn. And that's why I don't drive with her. My ears would bleed."

"You know you love them," she teases. "Don't let Coach keep you long, 'kay?"

"Can we go back to my house later?" he asks again; his voice hopeful.

"Maybe," she offers with a wink; not wanting to fight about it right now.

"Love ya." He presses a brief kiss to her lips before making his way back to the gym with a quick wave to Katie and Tanya.

"Jules!"

She turns from watching Stuart leave. Katie hangs out of the passenger side window, her hands raised in a silent question and Jules shakes her head; opening the door and sliding into the backseat.

"'Bout time, wench," Tanya teases, throwing the vehicle into 'Drive'.

Katie turns the radio down and twists in her seat. Jules can see what's coming from a mile away. She throws a happy smile on her face, but she's never been any good at fooling Katie, at least not for long. Katie's the analyzer of the group. You show up happy, sad, or angry, and the girl will pick at you until you tell her what's up in your life that's making you feel that way. She's also the psychologist; the one who will listen to your problems and give advice. Jules waits.

Katie pops a stick of gum in her mouth, a well-known stall tactic, before starting in on her. "What was up with Mr. Football?"

Leaning forward, Jules steals a stick from the pack for herself. A quick glance at Tanya shows she's busy playing on her phone while waiting to turn out of the school parking lot. Thinking she might be able to get out of heavy conversation, Jules lies. "Same 'ole, same 'ole."

"Ha!" Tanya bursts out. *So much for being busy.* "The boy just wants some action. I saw his grabby hands. You need to put him out of his misery already."

"Shh, she's not you, T," Katie chides; throwing an irritated look at Tanya before turning her focus back on Jules. "So tell Dr. K what's up."

"Oh, no you didn't. You did not call yourself Dr. K!" Tanya breaks out in hysterical laughter, earning herself another nasty look from Katie.

"I seem to recall having a thirty-minute session with you a few hours ago. Don't know what you're laughing about."

"If I knew it'd go to your head, I'd have asked Jules instead."

"Wait, wait—ask me what? Where was I when this conversation was taking place?" Jules yanks at her seatbelt so she can slide forward and get a better view of Tanya's profile.

"Boy issues as usual, no biggie."

"No biggie? And what boy? You've been playing the field all summer." Tanya throws her a look that clearly states 'shut it', but Jules isn't deterred. "Spill it!" After all, these girls are always up in her love life. She has no shame.

"Nothing. I was just telling K, I might actually be ready to try a relationship."

Jules nearly chokes on her gum. Tanya doesn't do relationships. She's the fun one. The 'let's party, kiss every cute boy I see, and who cares what anyone thinks' girl. Katie and Jules like joking about how Tanya's attempting to work her way through the football team. She's already made a descent dent on the O-line.

"And I told her," Katie interrupts Tanya, filling Jules in on what she missed, "that it was an awesome idea. Don't you think so, Jules?"

She doesn't miss the crazy look Katie throws her way. Trying to decipher the meaning, she quickly chimes in, "Of course. You know I won't argue with having a boyfriend."

"Speaking of?" Tanya pipes in.

"Yeah. What's up with you two?"

And . . . the attention is back on her. Throwing herself back into her seat, she slouches and contemplates her situation. Katie and Tanya have seen her through the ups and downs of her relationship with Stuart over the last two years. They always know the right advice to give, but lately things with Stuart have been strange, and she isn't sure if her two single-minded friends can help anymore.

"Nothing. We're good."

"Jules?"

"Don't 'Jules' me, Katie. We're fine."

"Leave her alone, K. They're the freaking golden couple," Tanya points out as she makes pretend vomit sounds. The sounds earn her a light slap upside the head from Katie, and Tanya jerks the steering wheel, yelling, "Hey! I'm driving here—watch it!"

"What about you, Katie? We saw a certain DB throwing you some serious 'I want you' eyes tonight."

Katie turns to the front, but not before Jules catches the dreamy look she gets at the mention of the 'DB'. The DB in question is defensive back Jeff Parker, Mr. Sweet and Sexy himself. They have a completely irrational relationship where neither one of them will man up and declare their coupledom, although everyone knows they're way into each other.

"There might have been some talk," Katie hints, and Jules leans in again.

"Yeah?"

"There's always talk, it's all you girls do. See why I haven't done the whole relationship thing? Too much talk and not enough action, ladies."

Jules rolls her eyes, laughing in spite of herself. "Good Lord, you're such a ho."

"Takes one to know one, baby."

"Whatever," she replies lamely.

All conversation stops as Katie squeals. She cranks up some country rock song she loves and starts singing along. The loud music gives Jules the moment she was hoping for to sit back and think.

She doesn't want to talk about Stuart with her friends because they're always on her side, and while she loves that about them, sometimes she needs to think things through on her own. This is one of those times. Stuart spent a good deal of his summer away; between football camp and staying with his grandparents in Houston, they've barely seen each other. In her heart she knows they've grown apart, and it confuses her that the reality of the situation doesn't seem to hurt as much as it should.

She's excited for school to start Monday so they can finally have more time together. Last year, after school and practices, they would sit in his car talking about the day and making out before he took her home. It was one of the few times during the week they had to themselves. In a town the size of Tyler, there's no such thing as going on dates alone. Everywhere they go, they run into friends. Plus, with Stuart, everyone wants to stop and talk football, college commitments, and Pro games on Sunday. It can be exhausting standing in the shadows while her boyfriend goes on and on about sports.

Yet, she does it happily. She's proud of him and of his talent on the field. He's on track to break state records this year. She shouldn't fault him for being preoccupied lately; his plate is full. She sighs, thinking about those kisses back at the school and the touch of his hands on her skin. Tanya's joke about him wanting action fills her head. So does his suggestion to go back to his place because his parents aren't home. She knows what he's hoping for, but she also knows he won't push her if she isn't ready. Maybe what they need is some alone time so they can work the kinks out of their relationship. Maybe if they're alone for a while, she'll be ready to progress their physical relationship.

Tanya and Katie's yelling stirs her from her thoughts. They're almost at the Shack. Her mind made up; she fishes out her cell and sends Stuart a quick text.

Jules: Let's go back to your house tonight. I want to spend some time alone—talking . . . and maybe a little kissing too ;)

She isn't sure how he'll take her text. It sounds as though she's offering up sex, and she fights back a cringe. Maybe she will finally do it. She doesn't know why they haven't already. Okay, that's a lie, she knows why—it has never felt right. No matter how many times they've talked about it or gotten close to it, when it comes down to it she stops him with a 'sorry' every time. And every time she turns him down, Stuart frowns while assuring her it's okay.

The sad thing is, sitting here now, she still doesn't get hot and bothered thinking about going to his place and being alone. She loves his kisses; she loves his touch too, but something is missing. Maybe tonight it's finally time to locate the missing piece. Maybe the piece is sex? After almost two years together, maybe they need something new to bring them closer.

Three

"How foolish it was to think I could solve my relationship problems with sex." She rolls her eyes at the absurdity before moving on. "Anyway." Jules smiles the memories of Friday nights, rushing in. "It was automatic for us to roll down the car windows whenever we pulled into the gravel parking lot at the Ice Shack. Windows down, radio up. That was the motto. Be seen, be heard."

Her head shakes at how silly they once were. Silly teenage girls, living life and having fun.

"I remember unlocking my cell to check for messages as the usual catcalls drifted through the open windows. Tanya loved being an attention whore . . ."

"Would you look at this place?" Katie buzzes, "Half the teenage population of Tyler is here tonight."

"Maybe we should start going someplace else?" Jules suggests; tapping out a text to her mom.

"Girl!" Tanya and Katie snap in sync, and Jules lifts her head.

"What?" She shrugs, catching Tanya's glare in the rearview mirror.

"After game tradition, remember? Senior year. We can't quit now."

Jules' replies with an over-exaggerated eye roll. Stuart's attitude is catching. *Didn't I fuss at him thirty minutes ago for making the same statement?*

Katie leans out of her window and waves at people like the Homecoming Queen she hopes to be crowned; her blonde bob blowing in the breeze and the over-sized cheer team bow sitting on top comparable to a crown. The girls survey the parking lot, taking in the many students from Hillsdale dressed in their school colors from the game.

"Crap, the Shack is slammed."

Tanya taps her horn as three guys walk in front of her car's path, causing her to hit the brakes and all three girls to curse as they jerk to a sudden stop.

"Move, Tommy!" Tanya shouts out the window; flashing her lights.

Muttering under her breath, Jules reaches down recovering her cell from where it shot across the floorboard.

"You've *got* to be kidding me," Tanya hisses; her fiery Latin heritage showing itself.

Curious, Jules peeks between the seats and is greeted with a most comical sight. Standing there in the beam of Tanya's headlights is Tommy Wilson, ever the showboat, dirty dancing. Tragically, his moves don't time well with the techno-pop song currently blaring through Tanya's car speakers. He lifts his shirt slowly, revealing some relatively nice abs, and waggles his brows, "Hey baby!"

A quick check of Tanya reveals a volcano full of anger ready to explode. Jules sinks into her seat and covers her laughter with a fist. Tommy certainly knows how to push Tanya's buttons, and right now he's pushing away, perhaps against his own safety as she revs her engine. He flicks his tongue out, licking over his lips, and Katie joins Jules in her suppressed giggles. Appreciative whistles and comments are thrown at Tommy from some of the guys watching the show as he continues to ham it up.

When Ruben spreads his arms and joins Tommy's spotlight dance, Katie laughs harder. "They're such idiots," she gasps; watching the boys' antics.

"You're not talking about me, I hope." A blond head pops into Katie's window and she jumps as Tanya lays on her horn.

All around the vehicle, shouts of laughter at Tommy and Ruben's dance moves ring out, followed closely by curses for them to move streaming from Tanya's mouth.

The blond is Jeff, a.k.a. 'the DB', and Katie's on-and-off-again boyfriend. His dimples sink into his cheeks as he peers around Katie.

"'Sup, Jules. Where's Stu?" He lifts his head in the patented boy head nod for hello. Before she replies, he turns to Tanya, "Knock off the horn, Ya-ya!"

Tanya earned the nickname 'Ya-ya' back in middle school when she accidentally flashed half the football team at a pool party. She dived into the pool and came up with her top around her middle. The boys, mostly immature seventh graders, came up with Ya-ya because they didn't want to get in trouble by calling her 'Ta-ta' or any of the more suggestive names they thought up. It took the girls a month to figure out what Ya-ya stood for, and by that point the name stuck. Tanya never minded much. She was proud of her 'Ta-ta's; both back then and more so now. She likes knowing the guys remember them.

With a disgusted groan, Jeff slides his head out of the window. "Dude! Move out of the way, T! Ruben," he shouts, before ducking back in and fixing his gaze on Jules. "So, where's Stu?"

"Coach held him back for a meeting. He should be here soon."

Tommy and Ruben finally saunter out of the middle of the parking lot, accompanied by applause and cheering, and Tanya turns her ire on the boy hanging in the window. "Hey Jeff, you wanna get out of my car so I can park now?"

"Nope!" He leans in further. Jules moves to the right, looking out of her window to see his feet come off the ground.

"Hold me tight, baby," Jeff orders Katie as Tanya rolls forward.

"Geez, Jeffrey!" Katie wraps her arms around his shoulders as he teeters on the door half-in and half-out of the car.

Luckily for him, Tanya drives into a parking spot straight ahead with nothing on the passenger side; otherwise he might have lost a leg.

"You're an idiot," Katie mumbles before her mouth becomes occupied with his.

With a groan, Tanya yanks her keys from the car, hops out and heads toward Tommy with purpose. Jules' eyes follow her as she walks up to Tommy and punches him in the arm. A scowl crosses Tanya's face as she exchanges heated banter with Tommy. His face, is the complete opposite of hers, as he keeps grabbing at Tanya's flying hands. Jules laughs when her best friend hits him again.

The unpleasant suck and smack from the front seat reminds her of the extracurricular activities going on, and she hurries to exit the vehicle herself. As she closes the door, her phone vibrates in her palm. She swipes the screen, expecting to see a message from Stuart.

Mom: Be careful and see you in the morning. What's your curfew?

Jules: Midnight, geez mom, I'm never late u know that <3

Mom: I know, just checking ;)

Jules: You know I'm a senior now i should get a later curfew, prepare for college

Mom: Nothing good happens after midnight, Jules. Plus, you're not going to college remember, you're going to stay home and be my baby forever

Jules: Not on your life! But i love you too

She hits 'Send' with a smile as she heads toward a group of friends a few spots down the parking lot. Sticking her phone into the waistband of her cheerleading skirt, she exchanges pleasantries with various students before stopping to talk with friends sitting on the tailgate of Ruben's truck.

"Where's Stuart?" asks Candy Crenshaw; her curly brown hair flying around her face in the light breeze.

"On his way," she shrugs. This is the typical hello she receives nowadays. Anywhere she goes, it's, 'Where's Stuart?' It's aggravating to be Stuart Daniels' girlfriend. She supposes it's harder being Stuart. After all, in the state of Texas where the only thing bigger than high school football is beef and God, being an All-American QB on his way to a second division-one state title makes you a celebrity.

Strong arms wrap around her body; locking her arms to her sides as the big body behind her lifts her feet off the ground and Jules yelps. Identifying the thick, dark brown arms squeezing the life out of her she howls, "Let me down, Ruben!"

"Shoot, girl! How'd you know it was me?"

"Dude, I can smell you. Didn't you hit the showers after the game?"

"Damn, baby. Why you gotta be so cold?" he whines; setting her down and spanking her rear as he asks the million-dollar question of the night. "Where's Stu?"

She spins around with a frown, but can't dig up the energy to yell at him. He's a three-hundred-pound teddy bear with a heart of gold. She repeats the generic, "He'll be here soon," and leans against the tailgate next to Candy's swinging legs.

Tanya, with Tommy following closely behind her, finally joins them ten minutes later as Jules and Candy are discussing the opposing team's cheerleaders.

"How do you play nice with them, Jules? That redheaded chick resembled a raccoon with all her sloppy eyeliner. I could see it all the way from the   stands . . ."

Candy chirps away as Jules notices Tanya and Tommy's linked hands. *T & T'*, she chuckles.

"This humidity is downright miserable," complains Candy as she keeps talking and talking, the constant droning turning her brain to mush. She switches her attention to Ruben and a few of the other football players the first chance she can, preferring to listen to anything they're saying, compared to the whiny, high-pitched tone of 'Randy

Candy'. The guys are engrossed in recapping their individual highlights from the game tonight, and she eavesdrops.

"That holding call on Marco was bunk, man. You kidding me? But when eighty-eight blasted D-man with that late hit? Nothing!" Grunts of agreement go out.

And so the conversations continue; on one side of her the girls' gossip, and on the other the boys compare game notes. That is until the deep bass of a rap song vibrates through the air and heads swivels to the black sports car turn into the parking lot, followed by a white pick-up truck. Tanya curses knocking into Jules' shoulder.

"Rossview players," she whispers, and Jules peers at the cars. How does she know who it is? She turns a raised brow to Tanya, looking for an explanation.

"That's Carter's car."

"Carter?" she mumbles thoughtfully. "Oh! Carter."

Carter was a summer fling Tanya kept secret. They hooked up back in June and had two hot and heavy weeks before BAM! they were done. Just like that. Tanya didn't mention him until cheer camp a few weeks ago, much to Katie and Jules' surprise, since they typically share everything.

The cars roll through the lot slowly, pulling up to where Jules and her friends are hanging out. All around the Ice Shack, people stare and conversations halt as the Hillsdale players realize who occupies the vehicles.

"Hey Ruben," the passenger in Carter's car calls, and all eyes go to the teddy bear as the person in the car waves him over.

"What? We played Rec together, don't get all excited."

"Hey, losers—go back to your own town," a voice in the crowd heckles, and the three guys sitting in the back of the truck behind Carter's car stand, their chests puffed out.

Acutely aware of the fight coming on, Jules removes herself from the over-hyped crowd. She makes her way to the Shack, approaching the window to order a cone before remembers her bag and money are in Stuart's car back at the school. Frustrated with how long he's taking, she stomps her way to the picnic table sitting to the side of the Shack, removes her phone and throws herself on the bench.

Jules: Where are you?

She stares at her screen, expecting a quick reply. It's nearly eleven o'clock. Too late for them to go back to his place now, unless she wants to break curfew. She's done it before, but hates to start the school year off in trouble if she gets caught. With a huff, Jules crosses her legs and flicks her long hair over one shoulder; absently twisting a piece around her finger as she scans the parking lot. The Rossview students are now surrounded by her friends. Ruben is hunched over, talking to the passenger in the sports car, and Tommy—with Tanya in tow—is laughing at Carter.

"Poor Tanya, that can't be comfortable," she mutters out loud.

"You always talk to yourself, cheerleader?"

Startled, Jules checks over her shoulder. "Excuse me?"

Sitting there, alone in the dark, is West Rutledge; his dark shirt and hair blending in with the shadowed surroundings as he gives her the once-over.

"You're excused, Buffy," he drawls; tipping his head to the side.

Jules fights the urge to laugh. She's barely spoken to West since middle school. Once upon a time they were friends, then the hormones hit, cliques formed, and West quit football. A Rutledge boy who doesn't play football is a rare commodity in Tyler, Texas. His father and two older brothers are all former Hillsdale players, and the middle son is currently a sophomore star at A&M.

"Does that make you Spike? Sitting here brooding in the dark with your flask?" she raises her brows with a nod indicating the small flask he holds.

A sly grin slips across his lips and Jules can't help but fixate on them as West takes a long sip from the flask. He's sitting on the opposite side from her, on top of the table, with his heavy boots on the seat. Clearly he'd been facing away from the parking lot when she first walked up, because while she noticed someone's presence, she didn't notice it was him. Now his body is angled toward hers, his arms resting on his knees as his flask dangles from his fingertips.

Shaking her head to remove the pleasant vision of his lips from her brain, she forces herself to look away, standing as she spots Katie and Jeff in the crowd. She barely makes out Jeff's raised voice over the crowd. He's between Tommy and Carter, a hand on both of their chests. A few steps behind him stands Katie; her hands fisted on her hips, looking pissed. Deciding to rescue both of her best friends from another Friday night fight scene, she steps forward.

"I think I could live with you calling me Spike."

The wind picks up and blows Jules' tiny skirt up in the back. Stupid outfits.

"Really? You do know Buffy and Spike hated each other?"

Does he truly feel that way about her? Sure they don't speak anymore, but she's never done anything to him personally. She's always nice to everyone. Her mission has been to debunk the stuck-up cheerleader stereotype. Lord knows Tanya and several of the other girls already have that market cornered. The lights in the Shack blink as West grins at her.

"At first," he points out; his voice dropping to what can only be described as stomach-flipping.

"At first?"

"Jules!" shouts Katie; jogging her way. "Can you believe this? Every freaking weekend they do this crap. Can't we just get Tanya and go? I'm so tired of all the pissing contests."

Katie grabs Jules' hand, tugging as she stands there with her eyes locked on West's.

"Oh," her brain realizes what West meant about Buffy and Spike. "At first." A blush creeps up her face as she recalls the way the characters got together in later seasons.

The lights flicker again and they glance around as the entire parking lot slips in and out of darkness. The air has thickened in the twenty minutes they've been there. A trickle of sweat runs down Jules back as her pulse speeds up.

"Come on," begs Katie.

"See ya around, Buff." West chuckles, giving her a small salute as he slips from the picnic table.

Jules can feel Katie's curious eyes boring holes in her back, and she turns with the intention of grabbing Tanya and leaving when all hell breaks loose.

Across the lot, Tanya's angry screams pull their attention. Tommy and Carter roll on the ground, each one taking swings, as Tanya stands over them kicking at their backs. The rest of the team stands by, watching. Perhaps they're waiting to see who has the upper hand, prepared to join in; if needed.

West mumbles "stupid pricks" behind her. They don't take a step before a shrill siren sounds into the night stopping everyone. Fifty teens stand in a gravel parking lot and watch as the lights down the street, toward the more saturated downtown area, flicker. Somewhere an emergency management message blasts on a car radio, but it's the loud, early warning siren that catches the most attention. In the oppressive wet heat of a late August night, the wind stirs and Jules looks at a pale Katie, as they both identify what is coming.

Four

Jules stops talking to the camera; pressing a palm to her chest as her pulse speeds up. Her heart pounds as though she's living the moment again. She's had enough nightmares over the months to recall every last detail.

Confusion turned into complete panic as people put two and two together. Shouts of "Tornado!" and "Run!" swirled around her. She closes her eyes, remembering the thick heat in the atmosphere. Opening them, she speaks to the camera.

"People ask how in this day and age a storm could catch our town so unaware. For those who weren't here, you have to know—there was no rain, no thunder or lighting; nothing that would have warned us of the fury heading our way. I think for the first minute when the sirens sounded, most people assumed it was a false alarm."

Jules and Katie stand rooted to the ground as a strong gust sweeps by, kicking up dust and flicking their skirts. In the distance a loud pop sounds, and the Shack is engulfed in darkness as the power goes out. Turning, Jules sees that the entire downtown is black. In the parking lot, headlights flip on as people jump in cars. Their wheels spit up gravel as they try to exit the parking lot, and the mass exodus causes a sudden gridlock while horns blare.

The sudden movement of vehicles jolts them from their frozen state. Katie clasps Jules' hand tightly. "Come on! Let's go!"

In a panic, Jules moves to follow her when a hand wraps around her other arm. Her head whips around at West's silhouette; his head shaking vigorously.

"No! We need to find a safe shelter. You can't outrun a tornado," he shouts, tugging her the opposite way.

"Katie!" Jules cries. She looks over the scene before them, taking in all of the other patrons and schoolmates scattering like ants at a picnic by foot or car. A deep rumbling fills the night air.

"Come on!" West pulls her arm again and Jules follows, dragging Katie behind her.

"Tanya!" Katie shouts. "Jeff!"

Bodies run every which way. The country road is filled with screams of terror, shouts for help and people telling others what to do.

"Get low!" Ruben shouts; coming up behind them and grabbing Katie's free hand. They are now a human chain.

"What?" Jules shouts over the noise.

"Get low! Remember the safety instructions? We need a ditch or basement."

The wind whips everything about. Jules' skirt flies up, her hair slaps across her face. Katie reminds her of Medusa, with her short hair flying all around her face.

The trees groan and snap as fierce gusts tear through them. The tornado is close. The telling sound of a train chasing after them fills the air. Generators pop off in the distance and Katie screams as something explodes. The blaring of car horns continues.

They look back at the damage and Jules makes out a large silhouette hurling through the sky toward them. It crashes to the ground, the metal scraping along the street, causing sparks as a car barrels into the trees across the street with a deafening crack.

The Ice Shack is situated on the outskirts of town, off the main highway but on a straightaway section containing mostly fields and farmland. There are two houses on this side of the street, and they run toward the closest; a sprawling farmhouse that's been vacant for years. Looking around her she sees the shadows of others running with them toward the house.

The sky is pure black, and with the city lights out, they're barely able to see two feet in front of them as they run. On her right, West's strong hand squeezes her fingers making them numb. On her left . . . no, her left hand is empty. Katie let go.

"Katie!" she screams, looking to her right, and stumbling when her foot hits a hole in the ground. West doesn't miss a beat, yanking her arm and keeping her on her feet.

"I've got her, Jules! Keep running!" shouts Ruben from behind. Katie reaches out her arm and Jules pulls back from West, attempting to grasp her best friend.

"Don't you dare let go, Buffy! We need to run!" West warns, yanking her back and into his side.

"I can't leave Katie!"

"We're not leaving her. She's with Ruben. Now come on!" His arm goes around her waist as he slows for a moment. It's enough to allow Ruben and Katie to catch up and he grabs Katie's hand as they pick up speed again.

The farmhouse comes into view and they run toward the front porch.

"This way!" West shouts, but with the noise behind them it's a whisper. Shadows of people continuing running past the house into the fields and some follow them to the porch. The windows and doors on the first floor are boarded up. Several guys run up, banging on the plywood and trying to break it down.

"What are we doing?" Jules asks when West loosens his hold on her and kicks the front door with his heavy boot.

"There's a basement here." He grabs her arm as she spins around and watches everyone trying to find a way into the farmhouse. "Stay by my side! Don't leave!"

"How do you know there's a basement?" cries Katie; hugging Jules with both arms now.

"I just do. Ruben, help me!" He punches Ruben's arm.

Debris rains from the sky and Jules finally remembers all of those tornado documentaries she's watched. She peeks back to where they ran from, and sees a mass of swirling black dust and clouds. Around her, people shout, as fists and bodies are thrown into the wood blocking the windows. Blocking their path to safety. Ruben and West ram their shoulders into the front door time and time again, to no avail.

"We're gonna die." She doesn't mean to say it out loud; it escapes her lips accidentally and Katie moans.

A voice calls out. "Help me! I've got it loose!"

West and Ruben push past the few others and rush forward with Jules and Katie on their heels. Someone has managed to pull a corner of the large piece of plywood on the corner window back enough to get their fingers under it. Hands go around the edges of the board and start yanking. Several people join in, trying to pull or break the wood free from the window casing.

"Watch the nails!"

They work together forming a human crowbar as they get their hands under the wood and pry it back, pulling until several nails squeal and loosen. Finally, they peel back a hole large enough for some of the smaller people in the crowd to crawl through.

"Katie! Jules!" Ruben shouts. "Get in there. Any other girls?"

A guy Jules recognizes from her science class smiles weakly at her as he pushes her toward the window. A younger girl she's seen around campus steps up with them.

"Hurry up!" demands a guy, pushing on them from behind. Panic grows within the small crowd. The wind picks up, the howling moving closer and closer.

"What's your name?" Jules asks the underclassman next to her.

"Lola."

"Okay, Lola. Crawl through there. There's a basement somewhere. You need to find it and go downstairs."

"It's in the back, in the kitchen. There's a door; you won't miss it," West explains and Lola nods.

Jules is curious how West knows exactly where the basement is, but lets it slide as she pushes Lola forward. Lola crawls through the gap the guys made easily, and Jules sighs in relief.

"Your turn," West shouts at her.

"No. Katie you go." She pushes at a crying Katie. "Go! Help Lola," she orders when Katie fights back, shaking her head in fear.

"Jules!"

Jules turns as Jeff rushes up, followed by more people. Katie is halfway through the hole when she hears his voice and flips out. "Jeff! Jeff!" The fear and shock in her voice breaks Jules.

"I'm here, K. Get in there. Go to the basement."

"Let me go in and I'll punch at the boards from the other side. We can't all fit through this hole," a guy offers, knocking into Jules from behind.

"Hey!" she barks as she's crushed against West's side. Pandemonium breaks out and Ruben and West lose their grip on the wood. Katie pounds against the plywood from inside, her voice shrill but drowned out by the commotion.

Behind them, the sound of the Ice Shack splintering into matchsticks jerks the crowd to a standstill.

"Oh. My—" Jules clutches West's shirt.

Shouts of panic sound behind her. "It's here!"

"Open the windows!"

Fists, bodies and feet pound on the windows and door again. Ruben, his face a mask of determination, throws himself against the house and lifts his arms above his head, pushing the plywood away from the window. West grabs the opposite side, pulling as they both shout for her to go in. Taking the cue, Jeff drags Jules from West's side and pushes her under Ruben's arms through the broken window.

"Tell Katie I'll be right there," he whispers in her ear.

Jules glances back at West and their eyes meet; a silent connection forming between them before she climbs through.

She stumbles to the floor of the pitch black house and breathes in the hot, stale air. The smell, a cross between a men's bathroom and a keg, makes her gag. A leg comes through the hole behind he and she quickly shifts out of the owner's way, kicking cans across the floor as she moves.

"I can't see anything!" she shouts into the darkness; her eyes slowly adjusting to her surroundings. "Katie, Lola?" Her hand goes to her waist remembering the cell phone she stuck there earlier, but it's gone.

"Jules?" a sniffling Katie answers. "Jules! We're over here."

Not much help in a pitch black house. Jules gropes blindly toward the person coming through the window to get their help.

He maneuvers his other leg through with a grunt and shouts, "Next!"

Jules grasps at his arm. "Do you have your cell?"

"You need to get to the basement, Jules. Not make phone calls." She recognizes the voice as belonging to Mark Jones, another football player from Hillsdale.

"Mark, we need light. Do you have your phone? We can't find the basement."

"Oh! Yeah, sorry." The few seconds it takes for his hands to fumble for his phone feel comparable to hours. The space glows dimly as his screen lights up and relief washes over Jules when he clicks a few buttons and one of those bright flashlight apps turns on.

"Here!" he hands her the cell. "Go!"

She ignores his order to go and holds the light up for Katie to see, "K! Can you see the light? Where are you?"

She shines the light around the vacant house and surveys her surroundings. She's standing in a large, empty room littered with beer cans and trash—thus the bar stench. There's a doorway straight back and another to her right. She can barely make out the balustrade to the staircase and what must be the foyer that way. "Straight or right, Katie? Which way did you go?"

"Straight! We're—right here, oh thank the Lord. There you are!" she cries; running toward Jules with Lola behind her.

Grabbing at her best friend, Jules yells, "Take this. Find the basement!" as pushes the phone into Katie's hand. Thousands of tiny clicks ping overhead; hail hitting the roof, she guesses, her eyes looking toward the ceiling. "Hurry up and go!"

"Not without you!"

Behind her, two more guys crawl through the window and, along with Mark, pound on the board covering the window from the inside. Nails shriek, popping out as the group makes progress opening a wider hole along the bottom and side of the window. The kid from her science class pulls out another cell phone, gripping it in his mouth as they break the board out more.

"Jules, I'm not kidding! Stu will have my head on a platter if I don't make you get to the basement."

It's Mark who yells at her, and she shakes her head, "I can't! I can't leave people out there while I hide."

The plywood cracks with a loud snap as it breaks in half.

"Go, hurry!" multiple voices from the porch yell at once.

Arms grab at Lola, Katie, and Jules, but she refuses—pulling back and fighting them off. Bodies dive through the window two at a time and Jules remains frozen, waiting for the faces she's most worried about to show up.

Jeff jumps through the window, cursing when he sees Jules. "What the hell? Basement, Jules. Where's Katie?"

"Someone grabbed her. Where's Ruben?" she barely recognizes her own voice.

"He's—"

"I'm here, baby girl," Ruben's deep voice calls as he hoists his body through the window and drops to the floor.

Jeff releases her arm and runs with the others who came in but don't know where to go. "This way," he yells, giving directions.

"Ruben!" Jules hugs him gratefully. "Where's West?"

Booted feet hit the floor next to her. "Hey, Buffy. Miss me?"

She nearly drops to her knees as relief sweeps through her body at the sound of his voice. She doesn't stop and think about what she's doing, she lets go of Ruben and flings herself into West's chest. His arms encircle her, his lips pressing the top of her head. "Basement," he whispers, practically carrying her with him.

"Is everyone in? Everyone who was out there?" Jules asks as they locate the kitchen and follow Ruben down a steep staircase to the basement.

"The porch was empty."

Jules thinks about that. She doesn't think more than twenty or so people climbed through the window. Three girls. Where are the rest of the people from the parking lot? Did they find a safe place? Did they run? Tanya, Candy, Tommy, Carter? Where's Stuart? Is her family safe? Her brain runs in circles and shock sets in as West lugs her into the dark basement.

There's a group huddled in one corner with their cell phones lit, and she scans the crowd—science class guy, two guys from the football team, a face she doesn't know. In another corner she spots Lola with Mark, a basketball player named Simon and a junior she knows from the Debate team. West steers her into the back of the basement where she spots Katie, Jeff and Ruben. She thinks they're heading to sit with them, but he veers to the left to an empty corner. They're almost there when the train sound from outside becomes deafening and the house above them groans and creaks as the sound of demolition fills the air. West practically throws Jules into the corner; landing on her as an ear-splitting crash sounds above them. Dust and debris fall into the basement and something heavy lands on her leg. She curls up as tightly as she can with West on top of her, as the house over their heads lifts and falls, shattering to pieces all around them.

Five

"There's no way to describe the sound of a building falling to pieces above your head. The snapping of wood, the shattering of glass—it can't be described. I could barely comprehend the terror around me."

A tear slides along her cheek as she closes her eyes reliving the moments—hearing the panic-filled screams in her memory. They rise through the air, joining with the cacophony of sounds, from the howling winds of the twister as it passes over them, to the sirens in the distance.

"West was laying half on top of me. He'd flung me down on the hard concrete floor, and threw himself over me for protection. It's all a blur, but when we balled up as the house began to come down, I remember our hands were still joined." She lifts her hand, as if to show it to the camera. "The good Lord knows I clutched his hand tighter than a life preserver."

"It gets a little crazy here. I remember using my free hand to cover my face as I made myself as small as I possibly could. There was something heavy on my lower leg and in my position, with West on top of me and the way I was laying on my side, I couldn't seem to kick it off. Just as I was about to freak out, things changed . . ."

The house moans as an ear-splitting crack rips through the dark. Dirt, debris, and the house fall into the basement; landing on Jules and all of the other students seeking refuge there.

She has no idea what's happening, as she listens to things flying around and crashing. The vociferous sounds of the twister die down, the air eerily quiet compared to a moment ago. The tornado siren is no longer going off, she realizes. There are car alarms in the distance and more blasts, but she can't hear the siren and that scares the hell out of her.

"Everyone okay?"

She doesn't know who yells it first, but as the sounds above ground dissipate, the sounds from where they are grow more terrifying.

A girl cries, and there are moans, curses, and screams for help. Someone prays.

"We're going to be buried alive!" the girl wails, and Jules knows it's Lola.

Someone shouts for help and soon the others join in.

"We can't panic," West mutters with a cough, then stronger and louder, he yells, "We can't panic! Stop and listen!"

Jules flinches at the loud shouts in her ear.

"Sorry," he whispers; his face brushing her cheek. "Are you okay?"

Her head pounds and she feels sick to her stomach, but she nods and squeezes his hand once letting him know she hears him.

"Yo!" Ruben's voice rises above the rest and echoes off the walls. "Chill out, everyone."

The voices die down until there are only a few sniffles and hiccups, and the shifting of whatever has fallen into the basement.

"Jeff?" West shouts, his voice carrying a note of uncertainty.

"I'm good man, and so is Katie." Jules tears up, grateful her friends aren't hurt. "Mark?" Jeff calls.

From there, a roll call takes place. Mark accounts for the people in his corner; Lola, who continues to cry, Simon and Debate class kid; she now remembers his name is David. She tries to remember who else she saw huddled in the corners when they came down the stairs.

Mark calls out more names. "Will? Tony?"

"Yeah man, we're good."

"I'm okay," another voice Jules doesn't recognize calls out. "I've got a Rossview guy here, though. I think he's knocked out."

There are sounds of shuffling, boards banging around, and something toppling over. Jules moans as the pressure on her leg increases.

West jerks at her strangled cry. "Jules? What's wrong? Are you hurt somewhere?"

"There's something on my leg," she grits between clenched teeth.

Lowering her hand from her head, she reaches out feeling around her. Inches above her face her hand touches fallen boards and sheetrock, and she swallows back her panic. Inches! Carefully, she stretches her arm in front of her, trying to gauge their position. Hope grows the more her arm straightens, then she stops. More debris. They're trapped.

"West? Are you up against the basement wall?"

"Yeah, I'm leaning against it. Why?"

"We're trapped. There's stuff everywhere in front of me . . . sheetrock, plywood . . . oh, no! The whole damn house fell on us, didn't it? How are we going to get out?" Her voice rises in octaves as she panics at their predicament.

"Jules!" She hears Katie's worried shout above her own whining. It's muffled through all of the debris, as if she's far away instead of in the same room. "Jules, what's wrong?"

"Katie! I'm all right, I'm not hurt," Jules shouts through the wreckage to her best friend. "How about you? You okay?"

"Yeah, I'm fine. I fainted. Where are you?"

"I'm with West and we're in the back corner. We're trapped under a bunch of debris."

"Hey, West, man—can you guys see our cell phone lights?" Jeff asks. He orders the others to hold up their lights.

West shifts and she flinches; nervous he might disturb things around them. "I can't see anything but black," he replies, and asks her what she can see.

Jules moves her head trying to look in all directions. "Nothing."

He mutters a soft curse. "Um, Jeff, we're pretty deep in the rubble here. We can't see a thing."

"Yeah, it looks like all the debris stacked up in the corner where you two are. We're pretty good over here."

"Good, then go get us help!" Jules orders.

"Jules, hun, you know I would love to, but the stairs are gone. We can't get out."

Her breathing speeds up as she pictures herself being crushed to death.

"Hey, hey," soothes West, his fingers touching her jaw. "Don't freak out on me, Buffy. We're gonna be fine. Our parents will be looking for us, and the cops will know to check the Shack."

Her breaths become harder and faster as she hyperventilates. "What if they're all dead? What happened to everyone else, West? There's only a handful of us down here. Where did they all go?" She breaks down, fear causing her to shake uncontrollably.

West rubs her arm vigorously, sliding down to her hip, and the side of her thigh. "Jules, you need to calm down. Slow breaths, or you're going to go into shock."

Her teeth chatter. "I c-c-a-a-a-n't."

"Dang, girl. I thought you were Buffy? You're ruining the fantasy here," he teases while his hand continues rubbing over her limbs.

"I'm . . . n-o-o-o-t-t-t. Wa-a-a-nt home."

"I know, Jules. Me too," he admits. "We're going to go home, I promise. You need to calm down for me. Close your eyes and try to breathe. Can you do that?"

Nodding, she closes her eyes and concentrates on slowing her body down; on being quiet. She focuses on West's hand maintaining its tight hold on hers—their fingers locked together similar to puzzle pieces. She lays there and envisions the strength he carries flowing from his fingers into hers, allowing his energy to fill her.

"That's it, keep doing whatever you're doing," he encourages. He shifts ever so slightly again—moving enough to put himself more behind her than on top. A board by their feet shifts, and she cries out at the pressure against her shin.

"Don't move!" she whisper shouts.

"I'm sorry! Sorry, is this . . . let me see if I can get whatever it is pressing against you off."

"No, no, no. It hurts and might collapse. Don't, please."

"Jules, I'm going to see if I can lift it with my boot enough for you to pull free. I won't move anything. We'll go real slow."

"I'm pretty sure I might pass out if you touch it, West. Please leave it."

Ignoring her, he pokes his boot around the area, the tread scratching at her bare shin. Jules bites her lip when he kicks the board that seems to be pressing against her.

"Damn it, you're taking this Spike thing too far!" she fumes, mad he's not listening to her.

"Ha, you know you like it, Buffy." He kicks at the board again and it gives. "Okay. Look, all I have to do is kick it and it's going to slide off easy, like Jenga."

"Jenga? This isn't a game, West. The whole thing could come crashing down on us!" she digs her nails into his hand to make her point, but he's determined.

"It's hurting you, I'm getting it off. Look, like I said, it's Jenga."

"Oh my word, what does Jenga have to do with this?"

"If you'd shut up I'd tell you, geez." He pinches her hip. "If the entire pile of rubble was resting on that board, I wouldn't be able to move it. Just like the game—how you move the easy pieces because it won't affect the pile—got it?"

"But what if you're wrong?" She wants the board off her leg, it's digging into her shin and hurts like all get out, but she doesn't want the house falling on them.

"If I thought for a second I could hurt you, do you think I would try this?"

"Ummm, I don't know. You're the crazy rebel, remember?" she points out.

"Wow, that hurts, Buffy. I know we're supposed to be enemies, but really?"

"If this doesn't work and that pile comes crashing down, I'm so hitting you with a stake to the heart." She moans pitifully, preparing herself.

"You already did, cheerleader," he acknowledges under his breath.

She freezes, sucking in a little building debris as she inhales deeply. With a cough, she covers her mouth and gives him permission to nudge the board away.

"On three I'll push it and you try to pull your leg out at the same time. Ready?"

"Mmm hmmm," she nods.

West's hand tightens around her, his free hand shifting to help cover her head. "One . . . two . . . three."

Jules' leg feels mild relief as his boot hammers small kicks at the board, moving it. With each kick his hips ram into her backside and he brings her closer to minimize the movement. Grounding out soft grunts, he kicks again and the board falls away. The pressure on her legs gone, she draws her knees to her chest, making a ball as the pile groans and shifts around them.

A few shouts sound around them and Jeff's anxious voice calls out, asking what's going on. Jules concentrates on staying close to West, praying they won't be crushed.

"It's all good," West assures them. "We're just making a little room under here."

"Making a little room? You mean you're trying to kill me?" she replies sarcastically.

"Why not? The way I see it we already beat death once tonight."

"West?"

"Yup?"

"You're not funny."

"You're not stuck anymore and you've calmed down, right?" Jules sighs because he's right. "Don't knock the methods if they work."

They lay there in silence for a few minutes. Through the debris she can hear the others talking and moving around. She crosses her fingers, hoping they'll figure a way out soon. Her ears perk up, are those sirens in the distance? She listens, her heart speeding up at the thought of help possibly being on the way.

Outside of their little space, Katie argues with someone. *What's going on?* Her mind goes back to English Lit last year when they read 'Lord of the Flies', and she imagines everyone stuck down here, jockeying for power. *Crazy thoughts*, she laughs at herself as she listens to the chaos.

"Just make me a base, then you stand up there and I'll climb it, Jeff. I'm a freaking cheerleader, I know it'll work," Katie snaps loudly enough for Jules to hear.

"It's a good idea," one of the guys agrees.

"And then what, K? Who knows what's out there, and I can't let you go alone."

"We need to get help."

"Hey, Jeff, you're strong enough, if we lifted you up after she climbs out, you could pull yourself out. We've got this. We'll get you both out, and you can get us help." Jules recognizes Mark's voice and calm demeanor.

"Okay, let's try it."

"What are you guys doing out there?" Jules shouts.

"We're going to get Katie and Jeff out of here so they can get help, Jules. We don't know how long it will take anyone to find us. Who knows what the town looks like, you know?"

If they're talking about climbing out of the basement, it means the whole house must be gone. She forces herself not to think about the rest of the town as she pictures the Shack being torn apart.

"Whose idea was it?" she asks, knowing full well Katie suggested it. Sometimes the guys don't give the little blonde cheerleader enough credit.

"It was all me, Ju-ju-be." Katie laughs. Jules frowns at the nickname being said publicly.

"Ju-ju-be?" West snickers softly behind her. "I like that almost as much as Buffy."

"Way to go, K. Be careful!" she calls out as she shifts her shoulders to speak to West. "And only Katie and Tanya are allowed to call me that, Spike."

"Duly noted."

"Did I ask you if you were all right yet?" Her head continues to pound and she can't remember if she checked on his health.

"Yeah, you did. I think I'm okay. I'm sure something took a chunk out of my back, but I can manage."

"What?!"

"I'm fine. It hurts and I can tell I'm bleeding, but it's not bad. I've had plenty of injuries, Buffy."

"We're trapped in tornado wreckage. Think you could stop making fun now?" she mutters, her voice hazy and drunken to her own ears.

"Jules?"

"I don't feel so good. I feel dizzy."

"Dizzy? Did you hit your head? Jules, are you sure you're not injured? Are you bleeding anywhere?"

"I don't think so. I don't know . . . my temple hurts, though. West, are we going to get out of here?"

"Yes, most definitely," he promises firmly. His free arm prods her head, his fingers running over her temple and forehead. "I don't feel any blood."

"That's a good thing, since you're an evil vampire and all." she murmurs, her voice fading away.

West growls, "Then you better stay awake, Jules. You wouldn't want me to take advantage of you, after all." His breathing picks up, his voice laced with panic as he shakes her arm. "Jules? Jules, c'mon now, wake up!"

"Buffy—" she reminds him as she loses consciousness.

Six

Jules wakes with a groan. As her eyes adjust she finds herself on a small hospital bed in the middle of a frantic triage center. The curtained wall surrounding her is open at her feet, a nurse's station sits across from her in the center of a large room.

She lifts her head slowly, surveying her condition. It it must be good if she isn't hooked up to any needles or monitoring equipment. Her clothes are covered in dirt and dust. Her legs and arms are covered in scratches, and as she lifts her leg she sees her shin is already turning black where the board landed on her. Laying her head back on the pillow propped behind her, she swallows hard. Her head throbs and her stomach is weak, but other than that she thinks she's all right.

She works to recall what happened and how she ended up here. She remembers the tornado, and running to the basement with West, and her friends. She recalls the building falling on them, and . . . nothing. Jules glances around nervously, the pounding in her temple intensifying. Tears flood her eyes as her brain plays back the screaming voices her mind can't remember.

An older gentleman steps into view at the foot of her bed and smiles politely at her. "Ms. Blacklin, I'm glad to see you awake."

She can't place his face, but he's familiar. His clothes are covered in dusty debris, the same as hers, and he has a black smear across his cheek. He's a large man with tall, broad shoulders and muscular arms that twitch as he crosses them over his chest.

"I'm West's father. I helped a crew pull the two of you out of the old Grier house."

"You did?" She'd met Mr. Rutledge years ago. "I don't remember anything. Where's West, Katie—my other friends?" She breaks down;

big, hot, fat tears falling onto her cheeks as she whispers, "Are my parents here?"

Mr. Rutledge seems uncomfortable as he watches her breakdown.

"Dad?" She covers her mouth at West's voice, watching as Mr. Rutledge tugs the curtain back so West can see him.

"Over here, son."

"This place is crazy. Did you find—" He appears around the flimsy fabric curtain and stops, relief washing over his features. "—Jules."

"Hi." She sniffs, wiping tears from her face with her palms.

"How are we doing here?" asks a young nurse, or maybe she's a Doctor, Jules can't tell. She has her dark brown hair pulled back in a ponytail, making her barely look old enough to be out of college. "I'm Dr. Metzger. I examined you when you were brought in. How are you feeling, Jules?"

"I guess all right. Um, my vision's a little blurry and my head hurts."

"Yes, that's to be expected. You have a concussion, so you're going to have problems with feeling dizzy, as well as spotty vision for a week or so. The good thing is you will heal, and you'll be okay. You're very lucky. From what I hear, you were buried under a lot of rubble." She smiles, looking between Jules, West, and his father.

"Doctor? Um, I can't remember any of it. Is that normal with concussions?"

West's face falls when she mentions having memory loss. His father's arm rests on his shoulder, giving me squeeze.

"Can't remember, huh? Okay, tell me what you recall last?" Dr. Metzger asks as she waves a pocket light in Jules' eyes.

"The last thing I recall is West," she gives him a small smile, meeting his eyes briefly, "pushing me down and dropping on top of me as the house started to fall. It's all a blur from there. I remember my friends, and screaming, and I heard a siren and voices yelling, but nothing is clear."

Dr. Metzger picks up the chart from the end of her bed and makes some notes. Turning to West's dad, she asks about Jules' parents.

"They're not here, yet. I don't know if they've been contacted. The lines are down."

Jules gasps and covers her mouth. "Where did the tornado hit? What's going on out there?"

"Hey—don't do that, Jules. Don't freak out before you know anything." West hurries to her side, reaching for her before he sticks his hand in his pocket instead. "Don't worry; we'll see if we can get to your parents. Dad?" he asks, his brown eyes pleading with his father.

Dr. Metzger pipes in before West or his dad can say more. "I'd like you to stay for a while longer, Jules. Just to observe you since you were in and out of consciousness for so long. As for your lack of memory, let's try to stay calm and not worry too much right now. Amnesia is common with concussions. Sometimes people forget a few hours, and sometimes they lose a whole day. Usually the memories come back after a few days, at the most." Jules nods, feeling less anxious about her condition now. "As for you two, I would suggest you stay off the roads and let the emergency crews do their jobs. We'll take care of Ms. Blacklin until her family can get here."

A series of beeps sounds and Dr. Metzger checks the pager at her hip. "I'll try to check back with you soon. A nurse will come by as well. If you start to feel worse, hit the red button. Okay?"

"Yes, Doctor. Thank you."

Dr. Metzger steps out of the small curtained area and stops by the nurse's desk as she goes. She waves back toward Jules' and makes some comments before hurrying to her next patient. To her surprise West sits, pulling the wooden chair beside her bed closer.

"How about I grab something hot to drink for us? West, how's your back, son?"

Jules studies West as he answers his dad. What happened to his back?

"It's fine. They used that liquid glue like they said they would. Coffee would be great right now. Jules?"

"Hmmm?" She's staring at his profile, trying to see his back, and has no idea why he said her name.

"My dad is going to get some coffee. Do you want some?"

Her nose crinkles at the suggestion but she nods her head to be polite. The only coffee she typically drinks comes from Starbucks and has chocolate chips and whipped cream, but she *is* chilly. Maybe something warm will help calm her.

"I'll be back." He nods.

Jules watches as he closes the curtain, giving them privacy.

"What's wrong with your back? Did you get hurt?"

"Oh, it's nothing. I guess something took a nice slice out of it, but they glued me back up and I'll be fine. They did have to give me a mammoth tetanus shot, though. I swear that hurt like a mother." He holds his hands up demonstrating the size of the needle, and she shivers thinking about it.

"I hate needles. Be glad you didn't need stitches." She fakes another shiver and West grimaces.

"Your dad seems nice."

"Yeah. You know he's my dad and all, but he's cool." She sees the look on his face. The look that clearly shows how grateful he is to have his father; to know he's safe. She can't imagine how losing a parent, let alone both, would feel. She imagines the thought ran through his mind at least once tonight. It's all she can think about right now. Are her mom, dad, and little brother, Jason, okay?

"Please don't cry." West leans forward in his chair and finally reaches a hand out to touch her arm. "I really hate it."

She lets the few tears run down her cheeks and attempts a small smile. "Your dad kinda freaked out when I started to cry on him. He must hate it too."

"It's been five years since my mom died. We've been a house full of guys and guy things. So yeah, he's not good with emotions."

"And you?" she asks softly, unable to stop herself. She's amazed at this new facet into West. He's been so aloof over the past four years. She remembers the funny guy he was in middle school when they all went to the same parties and hung out. This guy—the one she sees right now—reminds her a little of that boy again.

"I just don't want to see you cry," he admits, albeit uncomfortably, and rubs his index finger over his brow.

A chill runs through Jules' body. West's warm hand on her forearm makes her realize how cold she is. Her skin explodes in goose bumps.

She moves intending on bending forward to pull the blanket up from her waist, but West stands and helps her. He tugs the blanket up to her shoulders and waits while she settles herself. She rolls to her side slightly so she can look at him comfortably, and he returns to his seat and places his arms on the bed rail at the side of the bed; clasping his hands together.

"Does that thing move?" she asks, pointing at the metal rail.

"Uh, I would think so," he mumbles, looking around and jiggling the railing. He locates a button on the side and the rail slides down out of the way.

"Thank you. Do you know what's going on outside? What condition the town is in?"

"My dad said from what he could tell; the twister went straight through town. Apparently where we were, at the Shack, that might have been its last direct hit. It's still chaos out there, though."

She swallows hard. A burst of chaos breaks out outside her curtained room and West leans down, drawing her attention.

"Oh, I didn't tell you, we were rescued by Rossview EMS and Fire. They were closer to us obviously, so that's why we're here instead of at Memorial."

"I didn't think about it. I've never been to Memorial, either. So they're bringing a lot of injured here?"

"I don't know. I'm pretty sure they're bringing people wherever is fastest. It's really bad out there."

Jules nods, looking down at the hand she left outside of the blanket. She picks at the cotton, her nail following the cross pattern of the threads. Turning her face into the pillow behind her, she rubs her tears on the pillowcase as she breathes in deeply and attempts to keep herself calm.

"Hey, West? Do you pray?" she asks softly, lifting her face. "Like, to anyone or anything. I'm not saying it has to be God, but—"

His hand covers hers tightly and she stops speaking.

"I have been tonight."

She flips her hand over and laces her fingers with his, making a tight fist as she angles her head closer to his and closes her eyes. She prays for the safety of those she loves the most, for her parents, her brother, and her best friends. For everyone in the path of the storm tonight. She prays for all those hurting.

She doesn't know whether West prays or not, but he sits next to her silently and when she lifts her head, with hot tears running down her face, his is bowed. Looking up, she notices his father standing at the curtain entrance holding three cups—steam rising from them. Forcing herself to straighten, her fingers loosen their grip on West's hand, but he tightens, not allowing her to let go.

"I brought you hot chocolate, I hope that's alright. I saw the face you made when West mentioned coffee." He winks. She's hit with how similar father and son are. Mr. Rutledge's wink totally reminds her of West and the sly face he gave her earlier at the Shack before the twister hit.

"Thank you so much, Mr. Rutledge."

He nods, places her cup on the dinner tray to the right and hands a cup to West, as well.

"So listen, they're bringing in a lot of injured people. I ran into Chris out there and he said they could use help doing search and rescue. Since I have a four-wheel drive truck, I can get over debris." He watches West as he speaks, his face clearly questioning him.

"Go then, if you can help others. Do you mind if I stay here? I'll—" West turns to Jules with raised brows. "I mean, do you mind if I stay with you?"

"Of course not." His hand twitches in hers.

"I'll stay here. Then you don't have to worry about me."

"I think that's a great idea, son. Try to get a hold of your brothers if you can. They said the lines here are going in and out due to so much traffic right now. Jules, if you'll give me your address I'll see if I can get to your family."

"Oh, Mr. Rutledge! I would be forever grateful if you could. I—" She breaks into tears again. "I swear I only cry like this at chick movies."

West and Mr. Rutledge chuckle at her. "Your secret is safe with us."

"She lives in Hickory Ridge, Dad," West offers as Jules gathers herself.

"Hickory Ridge? Well that's good then."

"It is?"

"Everything south of downtown was spared, according to Chris. They should be safe, assuming they were home. They probably can't get to you or don't know where you are."

Before leaving, Mr. Rutledge enters her address into his phone. He promises to run by there as soon as possible and leave a note if they aren't home.

"You know, chances are they're moving Heaven and Earth to figure out where you are and get to you. The emergency broadcast is telling people to stay in their homes and off the roads if they don't need medical care." He walks over to West, who stands and embraces his dad tightly.

Although she turns her face away to allow them a moment, she catches Mr. Rutledge whisper something in West's ear and West nods in agreement. His father gives her a soft smile and tells her to take care.

"Thank you again," she calls after him as he leaves.

Jules blows on her hot chocolate and stares past her bed at the busy nurse's station. She watches as people, many wearing pajamas, run up to the desk frantic for information on loved ones. Every time a new person steps up, a nurse at the desk politely answers their questions and points them in a direction; their heads nodding sympathetically. She watches as one man gestures wildly with his arms; his ripped clothing evidence he'd been caught in the storm himself.

"What made you run for the house?" she asks West after a quiet period of people watching.

"Sorry?"

"The house? You knew there was a basement. How?"

"How sheltered have you been, Little Miss Cheerleader?" He says it playfully, but she can't help feeling as though he's making fun of her at the same time.

"The parties?"

"Of course. Everyone's partied at Grier house at least once. At least, we did before the police caught wind of it and the place got boarded up." West leans back and sets his coffee cup on the floor next to his chair before resting his elbows on his knees. "You never came to any of the parties there?"

She shrugs nonchalantly. "I don't party. Not like that, anyhow."

The parties at Grier house were known for the excessive sex, drugs, and alcohol being served up. Back when she was a freshman, she remembers hearing about a junior who got knocked up at one of those parties. Apparently they were raves for high schoolers.

"You don't have to get stoned or wasted at a party, Buffy. More people than you think used to come. We'd have a good time, hang, dance. Some people would smoke weed or drink, but it was cool to just chill, too."

"Illegally, in an abandoned house?" she rolls her eyes dramatically. "Do you know the crap I'd get in if I were caught doing that?"

"Oh, Miss Goody Two Shoes, that's why you make sure Mommy and Daddy don't find out. You know, your boyfriend actually showed up at one or two."

"What?"

"Just sayin'." He shrugs.

"You're full of it. Stuart never parties without me."

"Sorry to disappoint you, sweetheart, but like I said, a lot of people used to show. Ask Parker or Ya-ya."

Jules sits up and nearly pukes from the sudden movement. West pops up from his seat.

"Whoa. You're looking a little green, Buff. Sit back and relax. You okay?"

"Are you freaking kidding me? You don't hang with our crowd anymore, and here you are telling me you've been partying with some of my best friends. You called Tanya 'Ya-ya'. Where have you been for the past four years?" She's irrationally mad all of a sudden, thinking she's been left out of something by the people she thought she knew. Stuart going to parties and not telling her certainly sets off a red light, and Jeff—well, she recalls how close he and West were back when they played ball together, but Tanya? Tanya loves a good party, and they've gone to a few together. Jules isn't a goody-two shoes, regardless of what West might think. But for Tanya to go to Grier parties and never tell her?

"First, I was there the day Tanya was given the name Ya-ya, so I damn well have the right to call her that. Second, you're right. I don't hang with *your* crowd anymore, but I never left, Jules. I've been here all this time." Picking up his cup, he stands and runs his hand through his hair in frustration. "I'll be back."

Seven

She stops him with a question.

"If you didn't leave, then why did you stop being friends with us?"

His shoulders stiffen and he rolls his head from side to side. Turning, he opens his mouth to speak, right as a group of people come rushing into the triage area.

"I was told my daughter is here—Jules Blacklin?" her father's anxious voice says.

"Daddy!" she calls out at the same time West says, "Mr. Blacklin? She's right here."

"Jules!" Her father rushes to her side, practically knocking West over in his haste. "Oh, my baby girl. Thank the Lord you're alive."

Katie's parents pop around the curtain too, relief and worry etched on their faces. Her mom wipes at tears as she squeezes Jules' leg under the covers.

"Honey, where's Katie? Is she all right?"

Jules' dad loosens his grip on her shoulders as she explains the events of the night. How they ran for the Grier house basement, how the house fell on them, trapping her and West. She looks toward West, who maintains his position by the curtain doorway.

"I . . . I don't know where she is, because I blacked out. What happened?" she calls over the Luther's shoulders to West for his assistance.

"She was fine, Mrs. Luther. She climbed out of the basement with Jeff Parker to get help for us. I don't know what happened to them, I'm sorry. When they finally pulled us out, the others that were with us had already been taken away. They were worried about Jules, so they loaded her into an ambulance right away and brought her here."

Mrs. Luther lets out a small gasp and her husband straightens. "I'm going to go speak to the nurses and see what they can tell me."

Katie's mom digs out her cell phone, searching for a signal. "Are the cell lines down too?" Jules asks curiously. She has an overwhelming urge to call her friends and verify everyone is safe.

"The circuits are busy. I imagine they're overloaded right now. I wish I could get word to your mother. She was worried sick."

"You guys were okay at home, then? Nothing hit there? Why didn't she come with you?"

"We were fine. The storm looks to have hit right outside the elementary school and followed highway sixteen through downtown; passing by the Grier house and ending right outside the town limits in Rossview. Mom is at home with Jason. He's pretty shaken up, and we didn't know what kind of mess we'd find trying to get here."

"How did you get here? Mr. Rutledge was on his way to our house to let y'all know I'm okay. He said he didn't think you'd be able to get here without a four-wheel drive vehicle."

"Mr. Rutledge?" Her father's confused.

"Dad, you remember West, don't you?" she asks, pointing toward West, who is looking out at the triage area. When she says his name, he turns and nods respectfully toward her father. "I'm pretty sure he saved my life—and Katie's too," she adds with a smile toward Mrs. Luther.

Her dad walks over to West. "It's been a long time, West." His hand clasps West's shoulder much as his fathers did earlier. An embarrassed look crosses West's features as he stands there looking at her father. "Jules says you're a hero, huh?"

"Oh, no sir. No, all I did was grab her hand and run, sir. Anyone would have done it."

"He's being modest, Daddy. He threw me on the ground and covered me when the house started to come down on us."

"Oh," sighs Katie's mom; her eyes wide. "I can't imagine what you kids went through out there." Big tears fall from her eyes.

"There were only like, what, twelve of us in the house? Our friends scattered everywhere. We don't know what happened to them—" Jules' voice breaks as reality sinks in. "Mrs. Luther, we lost Tanya, and Candy, and Tommy. I don't know where Stuart is, either." Her voice drifts off and Katie's mom pulls her into a hug, crying with her.

Her father starts talking, she assumes to West. "We were able to get to the edge of Grier field. We had to drive all the way around the town and backtrack, but we knew you were supposed to be there. The place was swarming with cops and Fire and Rescue, as well as a lot of civilian volunteers."

"What did they say?" West asks as Jules works at getting her crying under control.

"They said there were several fatalities there, but they're not done combing the wreckage. Then they told us everyone they found was sent here. They specifically knew Jules was here."

She swears West mutters, 'Of course, everyone knows Jules,' but Mrs. Luther's mumbled words of comfort drown out most of what's being said.

"Steph, honey? Apparently Katie's in the cafeteria. They finally set up a waiting area for people not needing medical attention and they have her name on the list." Katie's dad practically shouts as he waves for his wife to follow him.

"Oh, thank you Jesus," she gives Jules one last squeeze. "Love you."

"Love you too. Give her a hug for me and tell her I'm okay." They nod and rush out in a swirl of relief at knowing their child is okay.

West gives Jules a look. "Uh, I think I'll go too and check in. See who's here and all."

Her father takes a seat on the edge of the bed as Jules works to get herself together again. "Is your dad coming back here, West? Can I offer you a ride home when we leave?"

"Thanks, but I'm good. He'll be coming back at some point." West explains how his dad was going to go by their house, and that he left to help with rescue work. He also tells her father what Dr. Metzger said about her condition. She sits there, staring as he talks about her. He could have left as soon as her father walked in, but he's taking care to be sure her dad's filled in on everything he's missed.

Her eyes drop to his hands at his waist. They're clasped in front of him, one rubbing the other. She's opening and closing her own fists as she thinks about their connection tonight. When she realizes he's speaking to her, she snaps out of her reverie with an embarrassed, 'Huh?'

"I said I'll see ya around," he repeats. His gaze is vacant when she meets it, as though he's pulled a screen over his brown eyes.

"Oh. Hey, Dad? Could you give us a moment?" she asks, and West's lip curls up slightly.

Her dad's confused by the request, but he presses a kiss to her head, "Sure, pumpkin. I'll go see if I can find out when we can take you home."

Stopping in front of West, he offers his hand once more. They shake and his voice is formal as he says, "Thank you, son. We are indebted to you."

The sentiment embarrasses West again, but he nods and gracefully accepts the praise. Her father leaves, pulling the curtain closed behind him, and once again Jules is left alone with West.

When her father and the Luther's first walked in, she hit the button to lift her bed into a sitting position so they could talk. She inspects the blanket covering her lap, picking at the cotton once more. She wants to tell West she's sorry for giving him a hard time earlier, but she doesn't know the right words to say. She keeps thinking about how if he hadn't spoken to her or grabbed her arm, she and Katie would have run toward their other friends and might not have ended up in the house. Who knows what would have happened to them then? He saved her life tonight. Her shoulders shake as the memory of the twister chasing behind them as they ran across that dark field comes to her mind.

Sitting forward, she brings her knees to her chest and presses her forehead to them as the terror of all of those other students screaming and the chaos in the parking lot replays.

The bed sinks next to her hip and she's pulled into his arms—his scent a mixture of dirt, sweat and antiseptic. It's that smell—his smell—that brings a memory from the basement forward.

He pushes her down as the house above them groans in protest of the approaching tornado. She strikes her head on the cement floor, but has no time to think as West lands on her and pulls her into an almost-spooning position with his body on top.

She hears her friends' screams and West curses; his breath blowing the hair at her face. She grabs his hand and shouts, 'I don't want to die!' as the sounds around them grow louder and louder.

"We're not gonna die tonight, Buffy. I'll be damned if I finally get the nerve to speak to you again, only to die in this place."

"You told me we weren't going to die. Thank you," she whispers as she wraps her hands around the arm he has stretched across the front of her shoulders. "I don't know what else to say, West."

He stiffens. "I thought you couldn't remember anything from the basement?"

"I don't, not really. That just came back to me all of a sudden." Straightening, he removes his arms as she continues. "Why? What happened tonight? I don't know how long we were trapped down there."

He shakes his head with a small smile. "It doesn't matter. We made it out, and that's all that counts, right?"

He lifts his hand to push the hair back from her face, when the curtain slides open and her father walks in, a nurse in tow. Popping up from the bed, West throws one last look at Jules and excuses himself.

"Hey, Spike?" She speaks to his back. He turns, his eyes dancing as he waits for her to speak. "Don't wait four years to get the nerve again." She adds 'please' in her mind as West cocks his head sideways and stares at her before nodding once and walking out of view.

"The nurse is here to check you out one last time, then we can head home."

"As you can probably guess, I was so ready to get home to Mom and Jason. I wanted to wrap my arms around them and never let go."

"The ride home was slow and difficult, to say the least. A lot of the roads were blocked off, and people had left their cars lined all the way up and down the streets. We ran into Katie and her parents on our way out of the hospital, and since they came to the hospital with Dad, we brought them home."

"Katie sat in the middle, between me and her mom. At this point, I think we were all in shock. Our arms were wrapped together and we clutched our hands tightly. She told me who all had been found so far, and who she saw at the hospital."

Jules swallows. "She also made me aware that there were still kids missing, and how you were one of them."

She stares at the camera and thinks about the names they listed off that night, but she doesn't say them out loud…Tanya, Candy and Stuart, among others. She forces herself to continue. "Being in the car, we were finally getting more information on what happened. According to the radio, most of the storm damage was confined to the business district and two neighborhoods. I recall sitting there numbly as they reported updated stats."

Jules mimics the businesslike voice of the radio reporters. "Remington's restaurant roof was pulled off, EMS is reporting three casualties and an unknown number of missing. Hillsdale High School has been leveled, according to Fire and Rescue. No reports of casualties there."

"We all gasped. Seriously—you could hear five people pull their breath in, all at the same time. Katie and I exchanged mirrored, bug-eyed looks of shock. Of course she looked at me and immediately brought up Stuart, and Dad reminded us the reporter had said there were no casualties. He told us to stay positive."

"We dropped the Luther's at home and pulled into our driveway fifteen minutes later. The sounds of emergency vehicle sirens droned in the distance as Dad held my elbow and walked me to the door. The minute it opened, Mom and Jason came running for me. We all fell to the floor, hugging and crying."

Taking a moment, Jules faces off camera. From where she sits, a large family picture taken two years ago is visible, hanging over the formal living area couch. A wistful smile creeps up her lips as she looks at Jason with his white-blond hair and the big gap where his last tooth fell out.

"You know, as happy as I was to be home and alive at that moment, I couldn't help thinking of all the people who weren't so lucky. I think about it constantly. When I went to bed that night, I lay awake and thought about all of you; all of the other cheerleaders, football players, friends from school, parents or lovers who might be laying injured—or worse—somewhere amidst the wreckage."

Jules admits something, as if telling a secret. "I couldn't help but think of West and how he called me Buffy. How he held my hand and saved my life." She nods almost dreamily. "Yeah, West Rutledge was definitely on my mind that night, too. Geez, I made it home and got to have my teary-eyed reunion with my family. But as I sat there with them, happy to be okay, I was also torn. I knew this event, this moment, would change me for the rest of my life. I knew I would no longer be the carefree girl I was a few hours before. I knew nobody would be the same after that night in Tyler."

She sits forward, perching on the edge of her seat and looking at herself on the television. Her face, the stoic, serious face looking at her, is different than it once was. She's seen so much; been through too much. She returns to the camera lens, lowering her voice a little, for dramatic effect. "You see, I knew everything was going to change because hell had come to call that night, and some didn't escape it."

Eight

"I'm going to take a moment." Jules stands.

Walking to the camera, she presses the pause button and releases a deep sigh when the red light quits flashing. She pulls out her cell, scrolls through her contacts to the number she needs and sends a text.

Jules: I'm making the video. It's harder than I thought.

She presses 'Send' and makes her way to the kitchen for a drink. Pulling her favorite tumbler from the cabinet, reminds her how her friends always laugh at her obsession with drinking out of double insulated tumblers with lids and straws. Everyone knows which drink belongs to her, because she never leaves home without her signature cup. Her mom loves it because she uses the same cup all day and doesn't dirty up ten, the way Jason does.

She smiles at the random memories and lets them ease the stress from her limbs as she pours sweet tea and takes a refreshing sip. Whenever she feels tight or overly stressed, she remembers the happy things. Some days are easier than others.

As she screws on the lid to her cup, the cell phone buzzes and she swipes the screen to check her message.

D.M.: I'm proud of you. It will be hard, but it will help you. I promise.
Jules: I'm trying
D.M.: I'm here for you if you need an appointment. Just call.
Jules: Thanks

She takes a quick bathroom break and returns to the front room where the camera is set up. After one last stretch, Jules presses the Pause button and makes sure the video is recording again. Satisfied it's on, she sets her drink on the end table by the chair and sits back down. Since her shoes can't be seen on camera, she kicks off her little ballet flats and curls a leg up underneath her to get comfortable.

"Okay, so I think I'll skip ahead a little for now. I can always come back. This is my story, after all." She winks at the screen with a grin.

"Oh, wait. If you were here, you'd be asking about two things right now. West, and when I first heard about you. Let me tell you about the next time I saw him, because that covers the part about you."

Exhausted, Jules barely takes the time to stand under the shower and allow the warm stream of water to rinse the dried blood and dirt off her body and down the drain. She doesn't realize how cut up she is until she's standing in front of a mirror reflecting her battered body back at her. Her cheek is swollen, her eyes are purple, and her arms and legs resemble someone who went into battle with an angry cat and lost. As she crawls into bed and drifts off to sleep, she wishes the few memories she does have could have swirled down the drain along with the water and grime.

She's lying in bed mid-afternoon Saturday, the sun peeking through a crack in the blinds, when the low murmur of West's voice, followed by a somewhat deeper tone, rises through the foyer and into her bedroom.

Although the doorbell sounded several times, she's ignored them, burying deeper into her covers. Her body aches from the ordeal last night and her head pounds something fierce. Her dad poked his head in sometime before the sun was up, kissing her on the head. The touch stirred her to mumble a sleepy, 'What are you doing?' He explained he was heading out to help do some recovery work in town, and Jules squeezed her eyes shut keeping the memories out and fell back asleep. An hour ago her mom came in telling her she made some chicken salad and it will be available whenever she's ready to go downstairs. Again she pulled the covers up and squeezed her eyes shut. She's fighting the reality of what she might have to face once she leaves the safety of her room, but she can't help it.

Hearing West's voice, however, puts urgency into her movements and she slides from the bed, her limbs turning to jelly as she stands.

"Whoa."

Jules falls back and sits on the side of the bed as her head spins and dark spots flash before her eyes. She decides the deeper voice speaking below must be Mr. Rutledge. *Why they are here?* Jules slowly pushes herself to a standing position again.

She manages to crack open her door when a broken sob comes from her mom. "Oh, dear Lord." The strangled words fill her with worry.

Jules rounds the corner; her head poking into the open foyer below, "Mom?"

Her mom is inside the door with her head bent low. Mr. Rutledge stands close to her, his hand touching her shoulder as she cries. To the left is West, his hands tucked into the pockets of his blue jeans. He jerks at the sound of her voice, his expression changing immediately; pain and sadness evident in his eyes.

Paying no heed to the tank top and small sleeping shorts she wears, Jules steps into full view and takes a shaky step; grabbing the rail to brace herself for whatever dismal news the Rutledge's bring into her house.

"What's wrong? West, why are you here?"

He stands his ground silently as she navigates the steps slowly; her eyes glued on her mom's back. It feels as though everything is moving in slow motion, as if her mom is ignoring her, but in reality it's a few seconds before she turns toward Jules. Her face is pale and her eyes are rimmed red as she brushes the moisture from beneath her lower lashes.

"Oh, honey," she takes Jules' hand once she reaches the last few steps. "I have some bad news."

The black spots show up again and Jules grips the post to the stairs. She feels a sudden urge to vomit and swallows hard as she beholds the three somber faces before of her. She barely feels her mom's arms wrap around her, pulling her snugly against her, as she meets West's gaze again. Something in his look instinctively tells her what she's about to hear. His eyes lock with hers, his expression filled with indescribable emotions. There's deep sadness, but there's something more; something that makes her whole body tingle with the urge to be near him.

"Honey, it's Tanya. She didn't make it, sweetie," her mom whispers into her ear as she tilts her head against Jules'. The words are fake to her; a mimicry of the teacher in all of those Charlie Brown television specials she's watched through the years.

"Wah wah wah wah . . ."

The sentence registers deep in her gut, but as her head swims and her feet give away, she stays zoned in on West. As she stares his mouth opens, and his face switches from sadness to concern. She registers his movement toward her as if she's watching a movie. She doesn't feel present in the room as he flings himself toward her. She processes her mom's worried shout in her head before everything goes black.

"What? What happened?" Jules asks groggily, coming back to earth. She shakes the cobwebs from her vision.

"Welcome back, cheerleader." West's face hovers over hers, his eyes convey worry, even while he smiles his brilliant smile.

"Honey? Are you all right? You passed out, but only for a moment." Her mom explains as Jules blinks, focusing on her whereabouts.

She's lying on the floor in the foyer, right where she stood moments ago. Her mom is in front of her, kneeling and gripping her hand so tightly it might fall off. To her right is Mr. Rutledge, and she wants to climb into a hole from the embarrassment. Then she looks up. She's cradled against West—his arms under hers as if he caught her mid-fall, her back and head rest against his chest.

"You saved me again." She says into his upside-down face.

The vision brings to mind the Spiderman movie where Mary Jane kisses Spiderman upside down in the rain, and suddenly she's flushed with heat as a blush works up her body at the thought of kissing West in the same manner. She removes her hand from her mom's and attempts sitting up on her own; allowing West to support her from behind. She sits forward enough to cross her legs in front of her. During the excitement of fainting and falling, her top rose exposing her stomach, so she tugs it down and places her head in her hands in a futile attempt to stop the drums banging inside.

"It's this concussion. Man, it hurts so bad," she moans; trying to explain away why she passed out.

Clearing his throat, Mr. Rutledge stands, the floor creaking as he moves. "West, I think we should let them be now."

Massaging her temples, Jules turns, looking between father and son. West is conflicted as he skims her waist lightly with his fingers. She feels the heat of his chest through the thin tank top she wears.

"Why did y'all come by?" The sound of her voice rattles her brain.

"Honey?" It's the soft, sad word spoken by her mom that brings the memory back.

"Oh, no . . . no," she moans, and bile rises in her throat. "Tanya?"

Her mom stares back at her, her own eyes drowning with tears, and Jules' body shakes with the realization that her best friend of over ten years is gone. Folding in on herself, her mom pulls her into her chest and whispers comforting words as West scoots out of the way.

Feeling his movement, Jules' arm darts out of her cocoon and pins his leg in place.

"No!" she warns, her head popping up from her mom's embrace and shocking everyone with her vehemence. "Don't go."

"Jules."

"Please? I need you here. I don't think I can do this without you." She trails off in despair, hating the sound of her plea.

"West?" his dad's deep voice warns.

"I'm not going anywhere," West promises. He takes her hand from his leg and grabs her hip, sliding her back into his arms.

Completely ignoring their parents, Jules wraps her arms around his waist with a sigh and curls her legs beneath her. She cries into his shirt, leaving wet spots on the cotton as the deluge of tears fall. West rubs her back in small circles with one hand while his other holds her head gently pressed to his chest.

Behind her, her mom finally speaks. "You look exhausted. Can I offer you some coffee?"

It takes Jules a moment to comprehend that her mom is talking to West's dad. After his deep 'Thank you', their retreating footsteps indicate she and West are alone. They sit on the hardwood floor of her foyer for an indeterminate amount of time before she's able to speak.

"What happened to her?" she sniffs, her face pressed to his chest.

He inhales. *Maybe I don't want to know.* But she does.

"I don't know. My dad was with the crew that found her and two others." His voice is ragged and laced with his own tears.

"Two others?"

"There are a lot of casualties, Jules. All over town." His voice sounds as broken as her heart as he explains some of the devastation. She groans again and sits back, her face inches from his.

"That could have been us. We could be dead right now."

West's hands cup her face. "But we're not. We made it," he insists, the intensity in his eyes reminds her how lucky they are.

"Yeah, we did." She breathes deeply and covers his hands with her own before adding, "But who else didn't?"

West's eyes water as they stare at each other. "I don't know. I'm just glad it wasn't us." His lip quivers, proving he's on the cusp of breaking down. "I know that's selfish, but I was scared as hell last night," he admits on a choked sob, bringing her back into his arms.

She has no idea how long they sit on the floor wrapped in each other's arms. She's relatively sure she's cried every last ounce of water from her body, though. Her eyes ache and her throat is sore. She can smell the coffee and hear their parents' low voices in the kitchen. When her backside goes numb, they shift to sit on the bottom step next to each other. She nestles her head into his chest and leaves his comforting arm around her shoulders. She feels the light trail his fingertips make along her bicep and she shivers.

"Did you stay at the hospital for very long last night?"

"Um, yeah. I stayed there pretty much all night. My dad was busy."

"We should have given you a lift home. I'm sorry." She tries to pull away so she can look at him, but he tightens his hold on her.

"It was fine, Buffy. I saw a lot of people come in. Jeff and I hung out for a while. I saw Tommy, Ruben and Mark. It felt good to see people coming in and know they were safe."

Her stomach flips when he calls her Buffy, and she listens intently. "Tommy? He was probably one of the last people to be with Tanya before she—" She stops short of saying died. She can't use those two words together in the same sentence. Not yet.

"He didn't know what happened to her. He said they were separated in the crowd. I wish—"

"What's this?"

She jumps at the sound of Stuart's raised voice, the glass porch door barely makes a sound as he opens it. West's arm falls from her shoulders and Jules stands as quickly as her jumbled brain allows her.

"Stuart!" She flings herself into his arms as tears fall again. "What happened to you? I sent you a text but you never called back, and the storm hit. I thought you were dead. Tanya's de—she's gone." She spews the words in rapid fire, as Stuart simply stands there with his hands wrapped around her waist.

"I'm fine, Jules. You thought I was dead? Are you kidding me? I was crazy worried about you after hearing the radio reports, but my parents refused to let me leave the house last night. I finally told them it was too bad and left an hour ago. The streets are a nightmare. Thankfully I saw your dad on my way here, and he told me what happened last night."

"Jules?" her mom calls from the kitchen. "Do I hear Stuart?" She walks into the foyer with West's dad on her heels. "Oh, Stuart! I thought I heard you. I'm so glad you're okay. Jules was worried sick about you last night!" She gives him a quick hug.

"I'm fine. I was worried about her," he offers, looking at Jules as she pulls back from him.

The five of them stand there in awkward silence before West finally speaks up. "Well we better get going now, Dad."

Stuart slides Jules to the side as West crosses the foyer to the door. For one, fleeting moment she thinks he's going to walk out without another word, but he stops and turns to look at them; his eyes reveal a world of hurt. Stuart's fingers flex in her side. Can he see the hurt on West's face?

"Take care of her," West tells Stuart; his face tight. "She got a concussion last night and passed out again this morning."

If Stuart acknowledges what West said, she doesn't notice. She's too busy staring at West, her heart picking up at the thought of him walking out her door. She wants to stop him; to reach out, grab his hand and pull him into another long hug.

The impulse makes her wince. That she can possibly think of him this way while huddled next to Stuart confuses the living daylights out of her, so she simply nods his way instead. She nods to acknowledge both West and his father, who is now holding the glass door open after saying goodbye to her mom.

"Thank you for making sure we got the news."

West nods stiffly, his eyes focusing on her hand firmly clasped with Stuart's. Her stomach rolls and she wiggles her fingers free; feigning the need to fix her hair. Stuart's arm goes around her waist instead, and she leans into him out of habit more than need.

"You take care, Jules." His father gives her a soft smile.

West's bobs his head one last time before he turns and follows his father down the path to their truck sitting at the curb. The whole time Jules watches them leave, she feels a tug at her core.

Fear.

For some strange and unknown reason, she's afraid. Of what, she doesn't know, but the moment West Rutledge is out of her presence, the feeling takes over. Suddenly, inexplicably, she wants—no, she needs—West by her side.

"Have you ever felt like that? Like the one thing you needed to keep afloat, to keep moving, just walked out the door on you? I have. Twice, actually. It's the most bewildering feeling, Tanya. Imagine my surprise as I stood next to the boy, who less than twelve hours before I was thinking about giving my virginity to, and BAM I'm smacked in the face by a freaking MACK truck named West Rutledge."

"In a matter of minutes on a Friday night, I lost my school, my identity, the security of my first love, the personality of my sweet fearless brother, my best friend, my town, everything as I knew it. Everything changed."

"Minutes—that's all it takes to change your entire life. How do you deal with that? Not very well, apparently."

Jules shakes her head ruefully as she recognizes she's gone off track. She takes another sip of her sweet tea and starts again.

"Sorry, let's not skip ahead. So there I was, standing with Stuart, who apparently hadn't heard of your death yet. He was sweet, T. We spent the afternoon on the couch, barely speaking as I sat in shock. I slept a little; my head hurt so badly. Jason came downstairs from the nap my mom forced on him since he'd been up, terrified, most of the night before, and my mom and dad sat him down with us to explain what happened."

"You know, for all the annoying things Jason used to say about you and Katie, he cried. He jumped to my side and hugged me something fierce, too. His small hands gripped my neck so tightly I thought he might strangle me. He sat between me and Stuart on the couch, holding my arm and watching television, until he fell asleep."

"Stuart left soon after promising he would call when he got home, and I had to remind him we had no phone service. He pulled his cell out of his pocket and we both stared at it; like how in the world can these things not work? He kissed me gently and brushed over my bruised cheek with his fingers as he told me how grateful he was that I was safe. We never talked about it, about what I went through, or what happened with him to delay him from reaching the Ice Shack before the twister. It didn't matter. None of that mattered to me anymore."

"I took the steps to my room slowly. I felt like someone who'd been beaten and dragged through the town. I could barely pull myself to my room. My body, my head, and my heart were shattered and tired. I remember falling onto my bed and looking at my alarm clock. It was a little after ten o'clock. Ten o'clock. Twenty-four hours ago, we had no idea of the storm heading toward us. At that moment, as I rolled into a little ball and allowed myself to shed a few more tears, I had no idea the storm was only the beginning."

Nine

"When all was said and done, forty-five people died. Forty-five. Twenty-thirteen and forty-five people can die from a tornado in the United States."

Jules bites on her lip. "I would have thought it impossible before it actually happened. Crazy thing is, it's happened several times in the last few years. There were huge storms in Joplin, Missouri and Tuscaloosa, Alabama that surprised everyone. Despite the early warning systems, modern weather forecasts, and all our technology, Mother Nature wins every time."

"I slept in Sunday, choosing to stay in my pajamas for the majority of the day, thinking . . ."

Jules is lying on her side across her bed, staring at the bulletin board over her desk which is covered in pictures of her friends, when the peal of a phone startles her. The house phone rarely rings, since both she and her parents have cell phones, but they keep the home phone for Jason. There's a knock on her door a few moments after, and her mom sticks her head in.

"Sweetie, Stuart is on the phone."

She rolls onto her back and takes the wireless receiver from her mom with a small smile. She pats Jules' head lightly and closes the door behind her.

"Hey." Her voice is hoarse from all of the crying she's done over the past two days.

"Hi, how are you today?"

Jules groans into the phone as her answer, and Stuart chuckles. It isn't meant to be disrespectful, and she knows that. It's awkward. All of it is. Nobody ever knows what to say to people when someone dies, and Stuart is obviously as uncomfortable as Jules is with how to talk about it.

"That bad, huh? It'll get better, Jules. My parents keep telling me that we should be grateful."

"I am," she mumbles half-heartedly, as she waits impatiently for him to get to the point of the call. She ignores the stirrings deep down that cause her to feel this way.

"Listen, I'm heading to Houston for a few days. The grandparents freaked out on my dad and want us to come see them."

"When?"

He pauses, and sighs. "Today. Right now, actually. We're already in the car."

"Oh."

"I'm sorry, doll. It was flung on me; you know?" He lowers his voice to a covered whisper, "You know my mother."

Thankfully Stuart can't see her face. She knows his mother, all right, and can certainly imagine how quickly she set to packing when she realized the twister was going to disrupt her normal social appointments and routine.

"No, I understand. When will you be back? Will you be here for—" She stops.

"We'll be back later this week for the funerals."

"Funerals? Did you know someone else that died?"

"Yeah, a lady who worked in Dad's office." Stuart's mom speaks in the background and he exhales. "Hey, I'm in the car with my parents. Can I call you later so we can talk more?"

"Sure."

"Jules? Are you feeling okay today?" His voice finally displays more worry than it did previously.

"I'm fine, I've been sleeping. I'm not as dizzy today."

"Good. I'll call you tonight, 'kay?"

"'Kay."

They hang up, neither of them saying 'goodbye' or 'love you' and Jules sticks her head under her pillow; falling back asleep again.

The presence of someone sitting on her bed wakes her. The room has grown dark, the afternoon sun no longer shining in her window. A quick peek at the clock by her bed shows it's after five o'clock. She's slept the day away.

"Hi, sleepyhead," her mom's soft voice whispers as she stirs and rolls to face her. She sits on the edge of Jules' bed, dressed in a black, flowing skirt and top with little black rosettes around the scoop neck. It's an outfit Jules picked out for her on one of their many mother/daughter shopping trips. It makes her look young and pretty.

"Why are you all dressed up?" Jules asks as she stretches, sitting up slowly.

"There's a candlelight vigil in Center Park tonight." Jules sucks in a breath. "You don't have to come, sweetie, but I'm going. I thought you might want to."

"What about Dad and Jase?"

She shakes her head and Jules understands. Jase can't deal with all of these emotions yet.

"I can stay here and watch Jase so Dad can go with you?" she offers. She thinks about the types of vigils she's seen on television and isn't sure she would be able to make it through something of that magnitude.

"I think you should go, honey. You can see some friends—grieve."

"What do you think I've been doing?"

"Grieve with your town, Jules. You're not alone in all of this. We are all sad and scared and trying to figure out what to do next, baby."

She takes a deep breath and pats Jules' leg under the covers. "Come on. Get a good shower, get dressed and come eat. We'll go together."

Two hours later they make their way to Center Park, which is exactly as the name suggests; a park in the center of the town. It isn't in the actual center of the downtown area, but in the center of the town boundaries; southwest of downtown by scarcely a few blocks. They have to park on the street because the parking lot is already full, and as they make their way toward the park, Jules is amazed at all of the commotion. There are television crews from both local and national news channels all around; their bright lights shining on reporters talking into cameras. Jules and her mom duck around one person giving an interview and find themselves standing at the edge of a sea of people.

They weave their way through the crowd and stop to hug or speak with various friends along the way. Jules is overwhelmed by the support and the sadness. Recognizing Jeff Parker's head above the crowd, Jules tugs on her mom's arm, interrupting her conversation with two crying woman from Jason's school.

"I'm sorry, Mom, I see some friends. I'm going to go up front some. Is that alright?"

"Of course, honey." She gives her a quick hug before returning to the other moms.

Jules keeps to herself as she winds through the groups of people talking and crying. She hopes if she keeps her eyes down people won't approach her, and she does her best to look anonymous. When she finally breaks through the human wall of mourners, she finds herself at the front of the park, where a makeshift memorial has been made to the victims. Her eyes overflow the moment they take in the sight. Spread out before her are flowers, teddy bears, shirts, pictures, burning candles, and much more—all in honor of the forty-five people who died.

Stepping around a family huddled and crying, she slowly makes her way around the circular memorial, looking at the pictures and trinkets people left. There are handwritten notes and pictures colored by small hands in scribbles; a Longhorns hat propped on a teddy bear holding a picture of a handsome, smiling man. She kneels taking a closer look and her hands shake as she recognizes him. She used to see him around town, although she doesn't know his name. She moves to the next picture on the ground and recognizes her face too; a waitress at Remington's who waited on her family many times through the years.

Rising to her feet slowly, Jules steps back. Hugging herself, she contemplates all of the faces of the deceased laid out before her. They're black and white, men, women and children, young and old. Death doesn't discriminate.

She finally locates Jeff standing with some of their friends from school, and is on her way to them when a strange, tingling rides up her spine. Rubbing her bare arms, she checks over her shoulder. Not seeing anyone, she brushes it off and allows two cheerleaders from her squad to embrace her as she meets up with them.

"Jules!" cry Alice and Rachel, who hug her tightly. "Katie told us what happened to you two. I can't believe this, can you?"

"Is she here?" she asks, pointedly ignoring their comments about Friday night.

She hasn't spoken to Katie since finding out about Tanya. Her mom called Mrs. Luther this morning once their phone service was up. She said Katie is doing pretty much the same thing as Jules; sleeping, crying, and sitting huddled in Jeff's or her father's arms.

Rachel turns Jules back toward the memorial and points to the ground, all the while chatting about the twister, but Jules tunes her out. Her eyes scan the crowd, finding Katie sitting on the ground in front of a pile of Hillsdale Mustang school gear. In front of her, Jules sees not only a mound of items for Tanya, but also for the other students from her school who died. Choking back a wave of emotion, she pushes past two guys and falls to the ground next to her best friend.

"K?"

"Can we go back somehow? This is a dream, right, Jules?" Katie speaks in a hushed tone and leans her head on Jules' shoulder without looking her way.

"I wish it was."

"I was mad at her—"

Jules picks up an envelope that blew off the pile and places it closer to the other letters piled around the pictures of their friends.

Katie sniffs. "When Jeff and I reached her and Tommy, they'd already started crap with those Rossview guys. I told her to quit and she snapped at me. So I stomped away."

"K, that doesn't matter."

"Sure it does. She always loved it when all the attention was on her, and it made me angry for no reason. I shouldn't have gotten so angry with her."

Jules thinks about Katie and Tanya. In the past few weeks they'd gone back and forth, trying to one-up each other during practices. Tanya could be hard to hang out with sometimes; she knows that. Even Tanya knew that. Katie wasn't always the easiest person to be with, either. They both wanted to be in the limelight. Jules remembers the way Katie hung out of the car window and waved at people when they first pulled into the Shack Friday night. She got a fair share of whistles and catcalls for it. It didn't surprise her that not twenty minutes later, there were two boys fighting over Tanya. What happened between Tommy and Carter Friday? Did Tanya say something to start them in on each other?

Jules weaves her arm through Katie's with a sigh. "That was one moment, K. Look at all of these people," she urges, tugging at her arm and knocking her shoulder with her own. "We are surrounded by people who lost someone. Look at this pile; look at those pictures."

"How is this real?"

Jules shrugs. "This is our town now."

Around them, people pass around white candles with little cups attached. Jeff kneels and hands them each one. They stay seated in front of the pile of Mustang items. A blue and white pompom is one of the many things there, and Jules reaches out and runs her fingers through the tassels.

Across the memorial pile, Jules watches as dozens of candles are lit. Slowly, the glow of fire spreads outward as more and more people light their candles. There are others sitting on the ground around the circle; an older lady with two middle school-aged kids and an elderly man standing over them with his hand on the woman's shoulders.

Her gaze roams the crowd until she falls upon a pair of familiar brown eyes staring back at her. Almost directly across from her is West. He watches her, his candle already lit, as he stands there in silence. A body bumps into his side and Jules moves her eyes to the guy next to him. She recognizes his older brother, Austin, as he leans in speaking in West's ear.

She can't believe her eyes, seeing Austin Rutledge here. He was a junior football star when she was a J.V. cheerleader, but he was always nice to her at events. He's a sophomore at A&M now, and must have driven home to check on his dad and brother.

"Jules?" Jeff's standing over her, ready to light her candle for her. Offering it to him, she stands and moves to pull Katie up with her, but she's already standing. Brushing the grass from her shorts, Jules looks back toward West. He' gone.

They stand in silent vigil, their candles glowing, for roughly thirty minutes before someone gives a speech somewhere in the crowd. Jules hears the faint promises of 'Rebuilding', and 'Our spirits are strong' being touted as a politician at a political rally would do, except there's no clapping or cheering for this speech.

Deciding she should find her mom, she gives Katie a firm hug as they both hold back their tears and promise to call each other the next day.

She's wandering through the sea of people ten minutes later when a voice calls out to her.

"Excuse me, Jules Blacklin?"

"Yes?" she answers; looking over at the stranger standing before her.

"I'm Jackie Faye from Channel Ten news. I was hoping you would allow me to interview you about your ordeal Friday night."

Jules freezes. How does this woman know anything about her? She peers out across the crowd behind the reporter, seeing a group of friends loitering nearby.

"I'm sorry, I don't—"

"Just a quick interview, right here." She waves her hand and a small light clicks on behind her as a cameraman pops up from nowhere. Jackie Faye sticks a microphone in her face with a huge, megawatt movie star smile.

"Can you describe your experience Friday night?"

Jules stands there, her hand automatically touching her face where she knows her cuts and bruises show, regardless of the make-up she used.

"I understand you were with four of the victims at The Ice Shack Friday, and that you were almost a victim as you took refuge in the old Grier house with other classmates of yours. Can you tell us about that?" she persists; her voice sickly upbeat for a woman asking about dead teenagers.

"No, I can't. I got a concussion and have very little memory."

"You've lost your memory?" Jackie Faye gasps; sounding as if she's won a prize. "You poor thing. So you don't remember the house falling on you? The hours you spent trapped by yourself?"

Jules wants to walk away, but somehow her brain isn't connecting to her legs so she stands there, mutely allowing this woman to continue asking rude questions. She shakes her head at the last one. "I wasn't alone," she mumbles, searching for an exit strategy.

"Well, Ms. Blacklin, who else was with you that night? Maybe they would like to talk to the cameras."

"I—"

An arm wraps around her shoulders and a voice speaks over her head. "She was with me, and no, I do not want to talk to the cameras. Excuse us," West growls; pulling Jules into his side and sweeping her out of the lights and away from the crowd that has gathered.

Behind her people start talking about the events, and she glances over her shoulder to see the reporter already asking new questions. Without speaking, West guides her through the groups of people hugging and whispering. Many continue holding their almost burned out candles before their faces.

Once they reach a small clearing he stops and drops his arm from her body, but he remains close as he asks if she's okay.

"I'm fine; I was ambushed, that's all. How do the reporters know about the house?"

He shrugs and his arm brushes hers as they stand there. Jules' unlit candle dangles from her hand, and she lifts it, studying the way the wax melted to one side.

"Do you think this helped?"

"Here." He takes the candle from her hand and turns away, tapping the shoulder of the closest person. The guy nods and Jules watches as West re-lights her candle and thanks the man before turning back to her.

"What's it supposed to do for us? The whole lighting-a-candle thing?"

"I know there are a lot of religions that use candles to remember spirits of the dead, but I don't really know why. For me, I think it's a nice way to remember. I look at it as a metaphor of the light that a person once was. It kinda brings me strength."

She takes the candle from his hand. "I don't feel strong. I feel alone and empty, like I want to crawl into a dark space," she admits, and a tear rolls down her face.

"You're not alone," he offers. Their hands touch as she reaches across her body with her right hand to take the candle from him. Instead of letting go, West wraps his fingers over hers, all the while keeping his gaze on the small flame. "I'll be your strength, Jules."

Her shoulders shake as she stares at his strong profile, lit by the mellow glow of their shared candle. She studies the strong contours of his face; his straight nose, cheeks that always carry a hint of red in them, the angular jaw line that is still soft, but shows promise of what's to come as he matures a little more. He's amazing to look at, and Jules feels safe standing next to him.

Safe. It's a word that never crossed her mind until Friday night. This boy has repeatedly gone out of his way in the last two days to protect her. *He* makes her safe.

"West?" she whispers, and he turns toward her. His right hand touches her left lightly. Their shoulders touch as he gazes into her eyes. They're inches apart, separated only by the candle held between them. As his body shifts, Jules spots her mom watching and she flinches, quickly pulling her hand from his.

West's face falls but he doesn't say anything. Releasing his hand from hers around the candle, he steps back once and blinks slowly.

"You know what? I need to run. I'll see you around." She nods as he brushes her upper arm once with the back of his hand and walks away.

Ten

"You know those scenes in movies where two people meet, instantly fall in love and have these visions of their whole lives together? I swear I had one of those moments as West Rutledge walked away."

Jules shifts in the chair, her body warming at the memory.

"Mom didn't say a word to me about what she saw, but I could see it in her eyes. She was worried. You know how my parents always loved Stuart. Being at that vigil wore me out. I ended up spending Monday and Tuesday sleeping and chilling with Jase. Katie and I talked a few times, but honestly, I don't think either one of us wanted to leave our houses. Everything in those first few days after the twister is a blur. Everything was so hard."

The brush of a cold hand wakes Jules.

"Jase?"

"Sorry, Jules. Can I sleep with you again tonight?" her little brother mumbles sleepily; already climbing into her bed and tugging the warm blankets away from her body.

"Sure, bud. Try not to hog the covers this time, though."

Jason has climbed into her bed for the past four nights. Saturday night he woke her not long after Stuart left, and she'd barely fallen asleep. His skateboard pajamas soaked with sweat and his face covered in tears.

"Nightmare?" she asked, totally understanding the look of fear.

He nodded slightly, his blond hair sticking to his forehead, and she helped him wipe down and change into fresh pajamas. Knowing how he felt, she pulled back her covers and offered to let him sleep with her for the night.

The simple act repeated itself Sunday and Monday night as well, and while Jules is a little tired of getting kicked and punched by her restless little brother, she's happy to have him nearby.

Jason is the baby her parents didn't know they could have. Born when she was seven, they tried for several years, all but giving up until her mom came to the shocking conclusion that her 'food poisoning' was in reality a pregnancy. He was such a pretty baby, and Jules pushed him around in his stroller for months pretending he was her personal baby doll. They'd always been close. She's so grateful her parents decided to forgo their usual post-game Friday night dinner plans, going home instead. Her heart stops every time she thinks about what might have happened if they'd been out when the twister hit.

Jase loves football so much he forces her parents to bring him to all of the prep games each week. For a while she thought they were coming to watch her cheer, but he made it clear she was merely a sideshow.

"Ewww! Why would we want to watch girls bounce around when there's a game on?" he questioned one night during freshman year, when she told them they should skip the game due to the cold rain falling.

"Bouncing around? Is that what you think I do?"

"You shout a lot, too."

"Nice. You know bud, one of these days, you're going to be happy to have girls bouncing and shouting on the sidelines for you," she teased, ruffling his silky hair.

Her little brother made a disgusted face before running off to play with whatever toys were his obsession at the moment. He was barely five at the time, but they taught him right. Football is King.

She recalls being upset when she was younger because 'girls couldn't play ball'. Some boys on the playground were talking about Pee Wee league and how they were going to get to wear real pads and hit people. Jules remembers her pulse racing at the thought of playing football for real, and not just with her dad on the weekends. She was so excited, she strolled over to the group and professed her love of the game, telling them she was going to sign up too.

"Girls don't play football!" they laughed, making her fume.

"Yes they do."

"No way. You can't tackle a boy. You're too little."

"My daddy says I can do whatever I want, and I tackle *him* all the time," she pointed out; her hands plunked on her little hips, her face full of defiance.

She snuggles Jason closer, remembering how she ran home that day and paced by the door until her dad got home from work. She rushed to his car in anticipation of proving those boys wrong.

"Daddy! Can I play football?"

"Well, baby, let me change first and we can play, sure." He smiled as he grabbed her by the waist and swung her up into his arms.

"No! I want to play with the boys . . . real football."

"Real football?"

"Yes!" She giggled and whispered in his ear, "The Pee Wee football. That's a funny name for football, Daddy. Isn't it?"

He chuckled, telling her he'd have to talk to her momma about that.

She can't remember exactly what her mom said about the request to let her baby girl play football, but she did remember being taken to a local cheer center that weekend to watch the competitive cheerleaders practice. They'd danced and tossed each other in the air, their little skirts flipping up. Their big bows and glittery outfits were neon signs to a five-year old girl. She was hooked from that day.

"Jules?" Jason whispers in the dark.

"Yeah, bud?"

"Was it scary?"

"It was, but I'm okay Jase. You don't have to be scared about it anymore."

"What if another twister comes? What if it hits our house like it did your school or the McDonald's?"

She sighs and hugs him close. She has no idea how to answer these questions because she wonders the same thing. Until Friday night, it never once crossed her mind how an act of Mother Nature could do something so horrible to her little Texas town. The west coast has earthquakes and forest fires; the south and east have hurricanes, and there are blizzards in the north. She's always felt safe in her isolated area of Texas; far enough inland where the hurricanes that do come ashore are typically rain and wind by the time they make it to Tyler. In her mind, tornadoes hit Oklahoma and Kansas. Of course she knows that *technically* they can get them too—that's why they have drills. They've had plenty of severe storm watches during bad weather too, but she never expected one to hit.

"Jase, you can't be worried that something bad might happen. I don't want you to be scared all the time."

"What keeps you from being scared? What kept you from being scared when you were stuck in that house?"

Her eyes mist over as she pictures West. He kept her from being scared that night. She recalls how the moment he left her house Saturday, she felt her fear rising up again. She thinks back to those few stolen moments at the memorial Sunday night when he told her he would be her strength. She's slept the majority of the past few days away, her head continuing to cause her pain, but every time she wakes West is the first thing she sees in her mind. His presence in all of her dreams, and nightmares, since Friday night keeps him in the forefront.

"I held someone's hand," she whispers, allowing herself to admit out loud for the first time how much that single act meant to her.

The room is silent for a moment, their breathing the only sound before he asks, "And that kept you from being scared?"

"No buddy, I was always scared. We both were. But holding his hand let me know someone was with me, we were in there together. I knew he would try his best to protect me, and he did. He gave me his strength."

"Who will protect me?"

Jules releases a strangled cry, turned chuckle, at his innocent question. "I will, bud," she promises; hugging him tightly and finding his hand. "And Mom and Dad will. We love you, Jase, and we'll protect you with all our might. Try to get some sleep now, okay?"

"Okay."

The conversation brings forward a memory. Suddenly she's transported back to the small space she shared with West for a few hours Friday night.

"I'm scared," she admits. She's going in and out of consciousness, and is doing all she can to keep from puking all over their small space.

"Why?"

"Why?" she asks incredulously. "Well, hmm—we're stuck under the rubble of a house, a tornado has hit our town, and we have no idea what's going on out there. Listen to all of those sirens. It sounds like a war zone."

"O, ye of little faith. This is nothing. I've got you."

"You've got me?" Her head swims in confusion. Is confused too?

"Yeah, Buff. I've got you. I'm here and I'll keep you safe. No worries, okay?"

She wants to freak out. Her arms are pressed tightly between their chests, his hand holding hers. She feels claustrophobic as she wiggles her legs around. Something on the ground cuts her thigh and she winces.

"Hey," he warns mildly. "Calm down. Breathe."

"I want out of here. I can't breathe, my head hurts and I want my mom and dad. What if they're hurt?" Her shoulders shake. "What's taking them so long to get help?"

"Jules. Baby, you can't freak out on me now, please. I need you to stay calm." His free hand runs up blindly locating her face and he cups her cheek. "Look at me."

"I can't—I can't see anything." She gasps and forcibly tries to control her breathing.

"Pretend, then. Listen to my voice and picture my face in your head. Picture the Ice Shack from before all of this happened."

Taking another deep breath, she visualizes him sitting on that bench outside the Shack; his silver flask lifting to his mouth, the sly grin on his lips as he looks at her.

"That's good. I can feel you calming down already. I told you we're not gonna die tonight. Trust me. Will you do that?"

"How do you know? What if—" His finger presses over her lips, quieting her protest.

"Because I've got stuff I want to do in this life, and I'll be damned if this is the end."

She grins at the bitterness in his voice; her teeth grazing the finger lingering over her lips. He brushes her lip softly as he speaks again.

"Plus, while I've always dreamed of dying in a beautiful woman's arms, this wasn't exactly the way I planned it."

"Oh wow, was that a pick up line?"

"No, gorgeous, that was the truth. I'd show you what I envisioned, but I don't think we have enough room in this little cave of ours," he teases, and Jules' face burns at the innuendo.

Slowly, her fears retreat to the back of her thoughts as this playful side of West comes alive.

"It's a shame our accommodations are so shabby then. Should I offer you a rain check?" she coyly teases back. Clearly she isn't thinking straight, to make such a comment.

"Hell yeah you should. I'm taking you up on that, too. No backing out now."

Oh my wow! The memory causes her body to warm, her blood rushing not unlike molten liquid. She needs a cold shower. Maybe that conversation is why West asked her if she could remember anything they talked about. She can't believe she flirted so openly with him. Stress is the only excuse she can make for herself as she grabs her new cell phone from her nightstand and checks her messages. Nothing. It's close to midnight, but she sends Stuart a quick text anyway.

Jules: I miss you. First funeral tomorrow. Wish you were here to go with me. Call me soon

Two two things hit her as she lays there in the dark with Jase breathing evenly beside her.

One—she didn't want to tell Stuart she loved him as she typed her text. Two—she wishes she had the courage to call West.

She lays awake in bed for a long time, her mind playing tricks with her heart. Every time she makes herself think of Stuart and what he's doing, she's reminded of West, and she longs for him. *How is he taking all of this?* Is she the only one lingering over every minute of their time together? They'd been trapped and were lucky to be alive—it's not as if it was a romantic vacation, so why is she envisioning his lips on hers every time she closes her eyes? Why does she suddenly remember their 'rain check' conversation? And more importantly, why is she dying to tell him he should cash it in?

Eleven

Jules fans herself and takes another sip of her tea. Memories of those early days and her strong feelings for West always make her blush. Telling them to a video camera for people to watch some day? That makes her downright hot with embarrassment.

"The first two funerals were the next day. They were both for students from Hillsdale whom I knew casually, and although they were extremely hard, it's what happened on Thursday that completely changed things."

Jules is only mildly surprised when he comes up behind her at yet another memorial service for one more student lost. She stands on the outskirts of the burial site within a crowd of Hillsdale students who are making it a point to attend the funerals of each Hillsdale student.

It's their way of honoring those who won't be able to enjoy a full life. There are eight in all; eight bodies recovered. Four from the group at the Ice Shack, two from their own homes and two more from local establishments hit by the storm. Today's funeral is for sophomore Quinton Marks; a promising academic who dreamed of becoming an engineer and going to MIT. *One more dream lost*, Jules thinks, as she listens to the eulogy during the service.

Quinton's parents huddle together as they sit in the front row at the grave site. Their heads bowed, his mother holding a white handkerchief to her mouth as she rocks herself. The older woman to her left clutches her heart and cries openly. Tears rise as she watches their grief. Her emotions swirl in confusion as she once again thanks God for her life while questioning why so many others died.

She diverts her gaze from the Marks, no longer able to bear their grief, and is startled when a warm hand slides into hers. It's a simple movement; soft fingers rubbing against hers as they fit around her palm and squeeze reassuringly. Today she squeezes back without bothering to look behind her to verify the owner. The same hand found hers at two other funerals this week; silent touches of understanding at the pain they are all going through. Silent infusions of his strength.

Today however, when the crowd disperses his hand remains in hers. Instead of taking his leave, as he did yesterday, he stands quietly behind her. As the students around them leave, several acquaintances note her arm stretched behind her. With sad eyes and curious glances, they smile, but nobody bothers to do more than nod and offer a low goodbye.

"Jules," Katie calls softly as she weaves her way through the throng of mourners with Jeff by her side. "Sorry we lost you in the crowd on the way to the site."

They hug, Jules using one arm since her other is being held, and Katie's eyes widen in shock. She gives Katie's arm a gentle squeeze of warning, worried what her friend might say.

"Hey, West," Katie acknowledges his presence, surprising both Jules and West when she wraps him in a hug.

Jeff follows suit with a warm embrace for Jules and a 'guy hug' for West. With the ice broken, Jules eyes West as he steps forward. Their bodies are so close they're touching down the length of their arms from shoulder to clutched hands. He's wearing his signature black combat boots with dark slacks and a dark blue dress shirt today. Although he obviously attempted to tame his thick, wild hair by slicking it back and to the side, a few black strands managed to fall loose. He pushes the hair back as the four of them stand in awkward silence, gaping at one another.

"You ready to go? Jeff's parents invited me and mom over for dinner, but we can drop you off at home on our way," Katie informs Jules as she wraps her arm around her no longer 'off-and-on' boyfriend. They're totally on now, and totally all over each other. Katie told Jules they decided they didn't want to waste any more time being stupid. When your life is spared, when you get a second chance, you plan to make the most of it. Jeff and Katie certainly stared mortality in the face and they were ready to live. She gets it.

West stares at Jules, waiting for her to answer, and she falters. She looks down at their hands without moving her head. She doesn't want to leave yet. She wants to talk to him, to stand in his shadow, to take in his presence.

"Ummm."

West angles his body toward her, bending his head lower and pulling her gaze to his. "I was actually hoping we could talk. I'll take you home, if you want."

She feels her lips form a breathless 'Oh,' and gives a small nod. Katie tilts her head in that special way she has, curiosity written all over her face.

Snapping out of her daze, Jules looks up at West. "Yeah, sure. I can hang around." She turns to Katie and asks, "You good with that?"

Katie laughs under her breath, and slaps a hand over her mouth. Her eyes shift around nervously making sure no one heard. Jules understands. Any moment of happiness is one more moment than the forty-five deceased have. It's a guilty feeling.

"You don't need our permission," Katie mumbles in Jules' ear, pulling her in for another hug. "You so better call me later," she orders; putting her face within inches of Jules and staring at her.

"Yes ma'am."

Katie stretches up, pressing a kiss to West's cheek, making him turn a deep red as he looks completely taken aback.

"I still haven't thanked you for that night," she whispers against his cheek; her voice cracking. "I don't know how."

Jules' eyes prick with tears when West removes his hand from hers and hugs Katie tightly. His eyes are fastened on Jules' face when he replies to Katie's comment.

"You don't need to. Ever." He steps back, keeping his hands on her shoulders resembling a parent reassuring a scared child. He bends forward so they're at eye level. "Okay?"

"'Kay," she agrees, and a small tear drips from her lashes.

He hands her back to Jeff, who mouths a voiceless, 'Thanks man' before they leave for their car.

West and Jules stand together silently watching Katie and Jeff leave. He runs a hand through his hair with a sigh before slipping his hands into his pockets. Jules feels his gaze on her and tugs at her dress, suddenly unsure of what to say.

"How are you?" he asks finally. With the toe of his boot he kicks at a weed that is growing faster than the rest of the well-manicured grass at the cemetery.

"I'm good," she lies, and gives a quick wave to some girls passing by. "I mean—well, you know."

"Yeah."

A million things fly through her mind. *Thank you again for saving me.' 'I can't sleep at night without thinking about it all.' 'I can't stop thinking about you'.* She wants to say it all and yet she can't. Or can she? Live, Jules. Be Katie and Jeff. Don't waste a day wondering what if.

She turns to speak at the same time as West.

"You ready to leave this place?"

Her heart sinks. They haven't talked yet. "You mean, go home?"

West smiles the same sly grin she remembers from the night of the storm, and her heart does a somersault.

"No, I'm not taking you home. I said I wanted to talk, didn't I?" He looks around. The crowd, with the exception of the family, has all but disappeared. The Marks kneel silently over the coffin, taking their last moments. "I'd just like to get away from all this—this death for a bit. You game, Buffy?" He holds his hand out for hers.

"Absolutely," she agrees as she touches her fingers to his.

They walk hand in hand toward the street running through the cemetery. There's another funeral going on across the way. *Who's it for? What happened to them?*

"Uh, I didn't really plan this," he admits awkwardly, pulling her from her morbid thoughts.

Looking up, she understands why he said it. Sitting in front of her is the black motorcycle she's seen West drive to school from time to time, and she immediately backs up with a firm shake of her head.

"Oh, no. I can't ride that."

"Sure you can. Come on. I promise I'll go slowly."

"West?" She gives him her best 'Are you flippin' crazy?' look. "I'm wearing a dress. Freaking A, you're serious, huh?"

He grins and wordlessly hands her a black helmet before he slides on the bike, twisting around and patting the seat behind him in a silent 'Let's go' motion. Reluctantly, she pushes her hair back and secures the helmet tightly under her chin as she steps closer.

"You really are Spike," she mutters, as she does her best to climb on without flashing her lady bits to the world. Once situated, she tucks her dress between her legs and West shows her the pegs for her feet. Thank goodness her strappy sandals are secured with a buckle around the ankle.

"Hold on tight, cheerleader."

"Where?" she shouts as the motor revs and vibrates against her bare thighs. West doesn't reply. Instead, he moves her hands from his hips and stretches them around his waist; pulling her chest up against his back.

One minute later, the bike turns out of the cemetery and heads away from Tyler. Various pieces of debris litter the fields as they ride by, but for the most part this side of town bears no resemblance to the disaster zone two miles away. Jules can almost pretend this is a normal August day. Almost.

They ride for twenty minutes down a county road before crossing into Suffix County, the breeze cooling her sticky skin. The wind whips at the hair trailing down her back—suddenly the gusts of air remind her of the tornado ripping and tearing at her. She closes her eyes at the uncomfortable feeling and tightens her arms reflexively around West's waist; pressing her cheek to his shoulder.

"Everything okay?" West shouts over his shoulder, one hand leaving the handlebar to touch her forearm.

She can't seem to make words form. The constant buzz of the wind across her ears brings on an eerie sense of déjà vu. When the bike leans to the right, Jules yelps before realizing they're turning. She keeps her eyes closed until West stops, turns off the engine and kicks the stand down.

"Jules?" His voice sounds worried and she feels him twisting around in his seat when she doesn't answer. "Hey. Seriously, what's wrong?"

Composing herself, Jules straightens her shoulders and shakes the fear away as she stretches her fingers. She gripped West so hard on the ride over that her knuckles are white from the lack of blood flow. She goes to climb off, but West catches the front of her dress and tugs lightly.

"Did I drive too fast? What's wrong? Tell me, please," he asks softly as he releases her dress and unbuckles the chin strap from her helmet. His fingers skim her jaw line and she tamps down the shiver his touch elicits.

"No, nothing like that—" Her words stop on her lips as he removes her helmet and tucks her messy hair behind one ear. "Um, it was the wind," she admits, lifting her hand to smooth down her hair as he watches.

"The wind?" His dark brows crease together in thought before they shoot up; his eyes wide with understanding and his mouth drawing in a deep breath. "Shoot, I didn't think about that. I'm sorry."

He turns back to hang her helmet from the handlebars and Jules takes the opportunity to climb off the bike as modestly as she can. Straightening her wrinkled sundress, she admires the graceful way he swings his long leg around the bike and stands. His golden brown eyes are focused on her while she flips her head upside down, fluffs her hair and combs her fingers through the tangled mass.

Her racing pulse slows as she takes deep breaths, feeling somewhat normal again.

"Seriously, Jules—" West gives her a worried look.

"That's the second time in under two minutes that you've used my real name today."

Her jibe succeeds in relaxing the worry from his face, and he stops her hand mid-fluff when she lifts it to her hair again.

"Don't get too used to it, *Buffy*. You look great, come on."

She follows after him, finally checking around to see where they are. "South Berry Farm? Why are we here?"

Cornstalks stretch out for miles and miles in each direction, and West leads her down a row into the maze without another word. The crops have already been harvested and the stalks are beginning to brown in some spots, but for the most part the field remains green. The corn grows a few feet over her head, and after a few minutes of walking she discovers she's standing in the middle of the crops with no exit to be found.

Stopping and releasing her hand, West tugs his dress shirt out of his pants. *Ummm, hello?* Jules takes a small step back. His fingers move to his shirt buttons and her throat goes dry. *Am I seriously about to see the famous Rutledge chest?* The Rutledge boys are legends in the amazing abs,

89

chest, and buns category—or so rumor has it. She hasn't seen West without a shirt on since their year-ending pool party in the seventh grade. *Damn shame.*

He releases the last button and tugs his shirt off, revealing a vintage tee underneath. She groans inwardly, and attempts to cover her disappointment as West bends down and lays the shirt on the dirt path between the cornstalks.

"Have a seat, Buffy" he teases with a bow, taking a seat next to the shirt.

Playing along, Jules carefully bends down and sits on his shirt with a smile. "Now what?"

"Do you trust me?"

She doesn't have to think about it. He saved her life. "Of course."

"Lay down. Stretch your legs out and lay on my shirt."

"Ooooo-kay." Jules does as he instructs, scooting down until her head rests at the top of his shirt and her calves brush the dirt. Crossing her ankles, she tucks her dress between her thighs holding it in place in case of wind.

West lays beside her with their shoulders touching, and Jules slides over when she realizes his head is in the dirt.

"Share the shirt! You don't have to put your head in the dirt."

He chuckles but angles his head toward hers and places it on the shoulder of his open shirt. Jules waits while he settles in before questioning him again.

"And?"

He sighs softly, which causes her to roll her head his way so she can look at him. His eyes are closed and a peaceful, relaxed look washes over his face.

"Now we breathe," he whispers as his hand searches and locates hers.

Jules watches his face for a full minute, and when he makes no effort to open his eyes or look her way, she moves her face back to the sun and closes her eyes too, taking a deep breath as she does so.

She doesn't know how long they lay there, both stiff as statues, stretched out on their backs, as the late summer sun burns her exposed skin with its hot Texas rays. She moves her left hand to rest on her stomach and ends up tilting her face back toward West's to prevent the sun directly overhead from burning white spots into her eyelids. Her ears pick up on the rustling of the crops as a breeze kisses her skin lightly. She hears the sweet song of a bird flying overhead, but that's it. Lying out here in the middle of a cornfield, she feels all alone in the world, except for the boy lying next to her, holding her hand.

She's half asleep when she feels his thumb brush circles along the palm of her hand. Her pulse kicks up a notch. Instinct sets in, her senses telling her someone is staring at her. Slowly opening her eyes, she finds West facing her, his warm eyes a mere twelve inches from her face.

He licks his lips, not in the sexy *'Look at my lips'* way some boys do, but more out of habit. Jules melts at the unintentional sexiness. Being naturally sexy is ten times more enticing than pretending to be sexy. His mouth forms a question while she lays there staring in fascination at his lips.

"Why did you wait for me?"

Jules freezes.

"At the house, when you were inside and safe," he clarifies, in case she doesn't know what he's asking about. "Why did you wait for me?"

Her thoughts, her breath, her heart—everything stops as she stares at West Rutledge, the boy who hasn't been her friend since seventh grade. The boy who first called her 'cheerleader' and 'Buffy' instead of using her real name five days ago. The boy who grabbed her hand and pulled her and her best friend to safety that same night, the boy who threw himself over her to protect her life with his own.

She doesn't have an answer for him, and tears start to build because of it. She has no idea why she stubbornly stood by the window and waited for him to make it inside the house before she would go to safety. She doesn't know why he wants to know, but she tells him the only answer that enters her mind at that moment.

"I don't know. Standing there, all of a sudden it was like—like the thought of anything happening to you wasn't something I could live with."

Twelve

For one quiet, scary moment Jules wants to take the words back. She knows she doesn't have the right to say what she said. She's taken, long-term boyfriend taken, and admitting to the inexplicable feelings West Rutledge brings out in her isn't smart.

The spark in his eyes tell her her admission touched him. The problem is, it touched her too. From the moment he gave her his little grin and called her Buffy in his sarcastic tone, she began to lose herself. She can't explain it because there is no explanation. Some things just happen.

"Why did you speak to me that night?" she asks, and now it's his turn to look away.

Sitting, he bends a knee toward his chest and rests his arm upon it. His other hand never lets go of hers, although only their fingertips touch now.

"You all but slammed the door shut on everyone when we started back to school in the eighth grade. Why?" she asks, staring at the black tee shirt stretched across his back and shoulders. She resists the urge to brush the specks of dirt away as she waits for him to answer her.

"A lot of things changed back then." He picks up a stone and absently throws it into the row of cornstalks to their right.

"I remember the last time we talked. I mean really talked." Jules smiles and sits up, folding her legs to the side and facing his profile. She let go of his hand as she gets situated, and grins when, once she's settled, he catches it again without so much as turning to look at her.

"Yeah?"

"Yeah. Karen Wade's going away party, July before eighth grade started."

He offers her a small smile of acknowledgment, a light chuckle escaping his lips, as he turns. "You remember that night?"

"Of course. You were my first real kiss."

"No way. I call B.S. on that."

"You can't call B.S."

"There is *no way* I was your first kiss, Jules Blacklin," he continues staring at at her incredulously.

Irritated, Jules tries to pull her hand away. "Yes there is, and you *were*, West Rutledge," she spits in the same tone he used. "Gimme back my hand if you're going to call me a liar." Jules struggles to tug her arm away again and pokes out her lip in a pout, but West resists.

"No."

"No? Damn it, West, let go of me."

"I can't," he grinds out between clenched teeth and she stops pulling away. "I can't seem to let you go, Jules. I can't stop thinking about you, and about those hours we spent trapped together." His voice cracks and tears spring to her eyes as his face falls. "Your hand was an anchor. *You* were an anchor. I had you to keep safe, and it kept me focused."

He inhales deeply. "Man, this sucks."

West rubs a palm across his red eyes and Jules leans forward; her free hand reaching across and touching his forearm softly. She lifts his hand from his face to stop him from covering the tears. Her own eyes overflowing.

"It does suck," she agrees, allowing her fingertip to brush his cheek.

West blows out a harsh breath before he hauls her into his chest. He rubs his cheek against the top of her hair and Jules' arms go around his waist as she ducks her face into his chest with a sigh.

"I spoke to you that night because I was tired of pretending to ignore you. I've never truly ignored you, Jules. Never."

They sit there, tucked into a ball without a word for quite some time. Jules doesn't have words to respond to what he said. She revealed something to him and he returned the sentiment. What do you say to that? She feels his chest quiver under her cheek, and the deep breaths he takes in and out as he works to calm himself. She's cried so many times in the last five days, she isn't sure how she has any tears left to shed.

Jules figures he's pulled himself together when he clears his throat and runs his fingers over the top of her head, combing through her long hair.

"So, I was your first kiss, huh? How is that remotely possible?"

She laughs under her breath at his awkward 'change the subject' tone.

"I don't know. I mean, I never paid much attention to boys back then."

"You've *never* paid much attention to boys."

"What? Sure I have."

"Ha." He eases his grip and Jules leans back at his laugh. "Not since Mr. Football moved here. Stuart had your attention from day one."

"Whatever. What? Were you stalking me or something?"

"I noticed you." He shrugs.

"Creeper," she teases, crinkling her nose. "Besides, that's not true. I went on dates before Stuart."

"Everyone knew those were mercy dates, Buffy. We all knew you were biding your time waiting on Stuart. He's your Angel."

"What in the world? You're so weird. What's up with you and *Buffy the Vampire Slayer*? You're a guy! Where did you learn all this Buffy talk anyway?"

Although they're no longer hugging, they remain close enough for Jules to gape at the red flush traveling up his neck and ears.

"Oh." she practically shouts. "Don't answer that. I already know—Carley." She does a little 'I knew it' wiggle when West's eyes roll in confirmation. Laughing, she teases, "Your little goth girlfriend made you watch it, didn't she?"

His shoulder bumps into hers. "Oh, shut up. It was tenth grade. What's your point?"

Jules falls to her back giggling as she envisions West Rutledge with his black combat boots, messy, devil-may-care hair, and sinful grin sitting in a living room somewhere watching *Buffy the Vampire Slayer* with Carley Raine. She pictures Carley in her mind: her jet black straight hair, purple lipstick, and depressing obsession with all things black.

"Let me clarify things. First, the guys I dated before Stuart weren't 'mercy dates'. Second, Stuart is not my 'Angel', whatever *that* means."

"You guys have been together for, what, two years? He's your Angel; the guy you're hopelessly in love with. Whether he's right for you or not." He mumbles the last bit, but Jules hears it and her curiosity wins out.

"Why would you say he's not right for me? You don't know him."

"Forget it. Sorry."

"Forget it? Tell me what you meant."

West pushes up from the ground in one swift movement. He walks up to a cornstalk and takes a swipe at it.

"I should get you home. I don't want your parents to worry about you."

"Did I do something wrong?"

"What?" He spins around with his hands stuffed in his pockets, his face a canvas of confusion.

Jules sits there, thinking about what West said. How he finally talked to her last Friday because he was tired of pretending to ignore her. She can't figure out why he would ignore her, so as she sits there watching him beat up the cornstalks, it occurs to her that perhaps she did something to make him dislike her all those years ago.

She can't recall a single thing she could have done. She remembers their kiss at Karen's party, which was the last time they truly spoke. It was during the game 'Seven Minutes in Heaven' and somehow Jules ended up with West. They were pushed into a small storage closet before she could refuse. Although, thinking back on it, she never tried to back out. She didn't want to. She'd always thought West was cute, and was nauseatingly excited to kiss him.

"Have fun, you two," Karen sings as she closes the door; leaving them with merely a sliver of light coming through the crack at the bottom.

She stands there in the dark, wiping her sweaty palms on her bubble skirt when West pulls out his cell phone. The screen illuminates the closet enough so they can see each other.

He smirks at her and raises his brows. "Wanna sit?"

Back then Jules thought he seemed so cool about it all, but her memory reminds her of his awkward stance and the nervous shrug as he slid to the floor.

"Sure."

"How's your mom?" she asks before thinking better of it. It isn't a secret that his mom was diagnosed with ovarian cancer the year before. Everyone knows it's fatal. Although she's fighting her hardest, the cancer keeps spreading.

"Oh, well—"

"OMG!" Because apparently it was cool to speak in text speak when you're twelve. *"I shouldn't have blurted that out. That was rude." She sinks to the floor next to him, miserably embarrassed.*

"It's fine. She's alright," he mumbles and touches her forearm lightly.

Jules looks up to see him smile and lean toward her. The screen on his phone dims in his lap and his lips part slightly. That's the last thing she's cognizant of before the light goes out and his lips touch hers.

It's a perfect, soft caress; his parted lips pulling hers between his, the tip of his nose skimming hers. The hand that touches her forearm moves down her arm to find her hand; their fingers weaving together.

Jules gasps. The urge to kiss West overwhelming.

"Wow, I can remember it so clearly, yet I haven't thought about it in years." She stands, brushing the dirt from her calves.

"Remember what?"

"My first kiss," she hints.

West's hand moves from his pocket to cross over his chest and rub his bicep. For someone who stopped playing football four years ago, he sure is in great shape. She walks to him and places her hand on his forearm in a mimic of his gesture. West's arm drops and he locks his dark eyes on hers as she slides her hand down his arm, searching out his hand.

They stare at each other and wrap their fingers together; their warm palms touching as their lips once did.

Her voice wavers as she speaks. "You held my hand back then, too."

"I know," he admits. "There's something magical about your hands."

If the memory wasn't so poignant, she'd laugh. Instead, her throat burns as emotions swirl through her. She leans in and rises up on her toes slowly. Her free hand closes on the hem of his tee shirt helping her balance and his eyes widen as she inches forward.

Without warning, West blinks and mutters a curse as he steps back from Jules. Shaking their hands apart, he clenches the hand she held into a tight fist and walks over to where his shirt is; bending to pick it up.

Jules remains there with her empty hand dangling at her side. Tears burn her eyes while shame burns in her heart.

"Let's get you home." He takes off, walking back the way they came and leaving Jules to follow without another word.

The ride to her house is made in silence. They have to take several detours around the midtown area to get to her neighborhood, and Jules looks forlornly at the devastation as they pass though. People litter the streets, rummaging belongings not one mile from her own perfectly intact home.

As they arrive at her house, she sighs inwardly. She isn't sure what to say anymore. She tried to kiss West. *Good Lord, Jules! What were you thinking?* He flicks the bike engine off, leaning forward and hanging his arms over the handlebars. She swings her leg off the bike, careful not to touch the tailpipe with her bare skin.

She removes the helmet, hanging it from the handlebars the way she saw him do at the farm. She stands there for a moment and runs her fingers up and down the leather strap of the purse she wears across her chest, waiting. When his eyes remain downcast and doesn't speak, she elects to leave.

Two steps away, she pauses and takes a deep breath. She opens her mouth to apologize when he speaks first.

"Where's Stuart?" His voice is flat.

She wants to cry out of guilt as she faces him. "His parents freaked out and took him to his grandparents' house in Houston for a few days."

"You're still together, right?" His eyes are sad. She knows he already knows the answer to that question, so she nods.

His head drops and he runs his hands through his hair before sitting up and sliding off the bike. Jules' hopes soar. West steps up to her and blows out a deep breath before taking her hand again.

"I won't mess with what you have with him, Jules. That's not my style. But—" She holds her breath at the 'but'. "I don't know if I can stay away from you. Can we be friends at least? I can't imagine not being able to look at this hand, even if I can't hold it again."

Jules nods again, unable to speak for fear of breaking down.

"Give me your cell."

She wrinkles her brow as she removes the cell phone from her purse and hands it to him. Jules watches as he silently types something and lifts the flap of her bag up and drops the phone back in.

"My number, in case you ever need anything. You know, since we're friends and all."

All she can do is mumble "Thanks". She's in shock at his request that they be friends. She doesn't want to be friends with West—does she? No. She wants to kiss him. She wants him to hold her close and keep her safe. Heaven help her, she's confused. His next question only furthers her confusion.

"Tomorrow is going to be hard for you. Will he be there?"

"He's supposed to ride with me and my parents. He'll be back in the morning," her voice cracks, as she holds her tears at bay.

West nods. "Okay then. I'll be there too." He leans down and presses a warm kiss to her cheek, which surprises her. "I'll be the one mentally holding this hand," he murmurs, and lifts her fingers to his lips.

"The magical hand?"

"Yeah, the very magical hand. I told you it was my anchor."

They stand there for a moment before he backs up one step, and another. Their arms stretch as the width between them grows, but their hands stay connected.

"I'll see you tomorrow, Buffy," he promises, and their hands pull apart slowly. Jules watches his fingers slide from hers as if in slow motion. She turns and walks to her front door, looking back once to see West watching her. When she reaches her front door she gives him a wave as he climbs on his bike and fastens his helmet.

While waiting for him to take off, her phone vibrates in her small purse. She pulls out the phone as West turns into the street. Swiping the lock key, she finds a text from Stuart waiting for her. She frowns. Another text. She hasn't spoken to him since Sunday. Three days. It's akin to a world record for them.

Stuart: Got some cool news today. I'll be driving back tomorrow for the funeral but might be later than expected. Meet you there?

Jules: Sure

She feels a nagging guilt in the pit of her stomach and adds an 'I miss you' to the end of her text. She has no idea what's going on with her and West, but she hates what she knows is happening with her and Stuart.

Thirteen

When he doesn't reply right away she walks into the house, kicks her dress sandals off at the door, and pulls her purse off, tossing it on the table in the foyer.

"Jules!" Jason yells as he runs down the stairs and throws himself at her.

"Hey, buddy. Where's Mom and Dad?"

"Out back. Where were you?"

"Just out, bud. What's for dinner?"

He shrugs and keeps his hands firmly attached to her hips.

"What have you been doing today? Did you get to see any of your friends?"

"No."

"No? Sorry, bud."

"It's okay, I didn't want to go out anyway. There's a twenty percent chance of rain today, with isolated thunderstorms moving in this evening."

Jules bites her lip and forces a smile as she messes with his shaggy hair. "There is, huh? Wow, you're getting good at being a weatherman. Maybe you'll grow up to be one."

"Maybe," he agrees with another little shrug. "Then I could tell everyone when tornadoes are coming before they come, right?"

Jules wants to tell him they did know, but he wouldn't understand. "Of course you could."

She leans down and picks him up in a Hulk hug, making him squeal. Once she hears his laugh ring out, she puts him down again; happy to see a smile on his face, if only for a moment.

"I'm going to go talk to Mom and Dad. I'll check on dinner."

"Okay. Tell them to come inside before seven-thirty."

"Seven-thirty?"

"Yep. Storm percentage moves to forty percent at seven-thirty," he calls over his shoulder as he trudges up the stairs.

Shaking her head, Jules walks onto the back patio where her parents are drinking wine and talking. Her mom gets up immediately, crossing over to pull Jules into a powerful hug.

"Hi, baby, you doing good?" she asks, placing a kiss on her head.

"It was good. A lot of people were there. Jase recited the forecast for me when I walked in."

Her parents exchange glances. "We know."

"Okay, well he wants me to make sure you come in at seven-thirty because there's a forty percent chance of rain. Does he not remember how perfect the weather was that night?"

"Hun, he's scared. He's young and doesn't understand."

"I know."

Her dad takes a long sip from his wine. His eyes are heavy; dark from sleepless nights and long days of recovery work. Thankfully his office building wasn't damaged, but their company gave everyone the week off with pay to help with clean-up efforts and be available for their families. He's worked from sun-up to sun-down all week. Her mom cooks meals for families who lost loved ones or who are in shelters while waiting on home placements. As she studies their tired faces, she wishes she could do more as well. She's so immersed in her own grief; she hasn't thought about what she can do to help others.

"I want to volunteer to help with rebuilding, or something."

Her dad smiles softly. "Honey that's great, but with your concussion and all the funerals, you really need to be careful that you don't overdo it."

"How about next week? After my next doctor's appointment and once the funerals are done? There's so much that needs to be done and I want to help."

"I'm sure we can find something for you to do. Let's get through this week and see what the doctors say. Don't forget you'll be starting school soon, too."

"Speaking of, have they made any decisions on that yet?"

"Not yet, honey. There are so many decisions to be made."

"At this point I won't be graduating until July." She's exasperated. Every day they push off the school year is another day into the summer she'll be in class.

"They'll make the best decision they can, Jules. You know, in Joplin they're still going to school in the mall."

"Well that might not be so bad. Imagine all the shopping I could get done."

"Just what my wallet needs," her dad frowns, giving her a playful wink.

"Oh! Before I forget, Stuart is going to meet us at the funeral tomorrow, so we don't have to wait for him."

"How are his parents? Did you get to talk to him?"

"Nope, another text." She gives another big sigh and her mom sends her a sympathetic smile.

"I spent the afternoon with West."

"Rutledge?" her dad asks, sitting forward and holding his now empty wine glass.

"Honey, how many boys do we know named West?"

Jules grins at her mom's reply. "Yes, Rutledge. He dropped me off."

"You should have invited him in. I'd like to see him again. To thank him," her dad offers.

"Maybe next time." She shrugs, standing. It doesn't register that she automatically assumes there will be a next time. "You know what? I'm gonna jump in the shower. I'm exhausted today, and tomorrow . . ." She trails off, glancing at the knowing expressions on her parents' faces. "Well, tomorrow's going to be hell."

"Alright, baby girl. I thought we'd do breakfast for dinner. I'll start the pancakes in a few minutes to give you time to clean up."

"Jason will like that." She smiles, leaving her parents behind. Climbing the stairs, she pokes her head into Jason's room and smiles at the mess he's made. He built a fort surrounded by pillows and blankets in the corner of his room, and she can hear him talking to himself and playing in there.

"Hey, bud. Mom's making breakfast for dinner. Why don't you go help her?"

"'Kay!" his little voice calls out from inside the fort.

Jules steps into her room and locks her door before stripping off her dress and turning the shower on. She looks at the pictures scattered on her floor while waiting for the water to heat up. Earlier, she pulled together piles of pictures for Tanya's mom to use at the funeral tomorrow. Scanning the floor, one catches her eye and she slides a few out of the way as she bends down and pulls out a picture from the year-ending sixth grade pool party. It was a group photo, and a smile crosses her lips as she surveys the assembled kids. There she is in the front with her arms slung around Katie and Tanya. The other middle school cheerleaders are lined up in the same pose on either side of them. They are surrounded by boys sitting below them and standing behind them, and Jules laughs at Jeff with his tow-headed spikes and Tommy with his signature crooked Dallas Cowboys hat. He's flashing peace signs on either side of Susan Madoff's head, and Susan appears to be yelling at him.

She looks back at herself for a moment. Her hair was lighter back then, and pulled up into a side ponytail. Of course, that was the style when she was twelve. She remembers the little black and white halter top tankini she wore as if it was yesterday. She loved that suit. Katie and Tanya, with their matching hairstyles, have their heads butted up against Jules and all three of them have huge grins on their faces. Always the three musketeers. Remembering the shower water is running, she puts the picture down when her eye catches sight of a dark, wavy mop of hair two heads over and behind hers. She could identify that messy head in her sleep. It belongs to West, and in the picture he's staring right at her with that half-grin on his lips.

Later that night, she's sitting on her bed looking through a few more pictures from the pool party, ones with West in them, when her mom knocks once before opening the door and walking in.

"Dad and I are turning in, pumpkin."

Jules gives her a distracted, "Okay."

"Whatcha' looking at?" she asks as she sits on the edge of Jules' bed. Her eyes light up as she picks up a picture. "Look at you. Look at all of you. When was this?"

"Summer before seventh."

"Did you talk to Stuart tonight?"

"Nope."

"Is there something going on with you two, Jules?"

"I don't know . . . maybe."

"Oh, hun, you've been through a huge, life-changing moment. We all have. Give it a little time."

"I know. And I know he's hurting too, but if I'm honest with myself, we were struggling before this."

"You were?" Her brows rise in mild shock at the confession. Her parents love Stuart.

"Yeah. Honestly, I think we're more friends now than a couple anymore. There's not much of a spark, and we've already discussed how we're most likely going to different colleges and neither of us wants a long distance relationship."

"Sweetie, that's a year away. Neither of you need to be thinking about it right now." Jules' face falls. Her mom's eyes narrow. "Unless." she prods, obviously sensing there's more at play right now.

"I feel so wrong for feeling this way. He's been the best boyfriend; respectful of me, gets along with you, with my friends, smart, cute. Everything I should want—"

"But?"

"But I tried to kiss West today."

"You what?"

Jules' hands cover her face in embarrassment. "I know, I know. I shouldn't have."

Her mom pries her hands away from her face and holds them tightly in her own. "Jules, why did you try to kiss him?"

"I think maybe he's crushed on me for years. Years, Mom. He looks at me and I melt. I know it's wrong. I have a boyfriend who I shouldn't be screwing around on."

"Ummm, language and explanation, please," she asks sternly. Jules realizes how crude her comment probably sounded.

"Not literally. There's no screwing of any sort going on, promise," she rushes to explain, and cringes because her mom hates when she uses crass words. "Sorry."

"Jules, I'll tell you what my mother once told me. Give it time."

"Give it time? That's your big spiel?"

"Yes. I know it doesn't sound like much, but it's really all you need. Honey, maybe you and Stuart aren't meant to be, and if you're not you'll know. West saved your life. Of course you're feeling something for him right now. Give it time. Allow yourself to get some sort of normalcy back, then you can make better decisions."

"Is it wrong for me to be thinking of him? Of West, I mean. Like, all the time?"

"Sweetie, they're your feelings, so they can't be wrong. It's what you do with them that makes all the difference, but you have the right to feel what you feel."

Jules leans in and hugs her neck. "Now those are words of wisdom. I love you, momma."

"I love you too, pumpkin, so much. Get some sleep. Tomorrow will be a long day."

"Yeah, I don't know how I'm going to do it. I can't cry anymore, you know. It's like I'm numb, but I miss her so much."

Her mom picks up the picture with Tanya and Katie making faces at the camera. "You'll always carry these memories in your heart, baby. As for tomorrow, you'll get through it. We all will, and we'll get through the next day and the one after that. This whole town will; minute by minute, hour by hour, day by day. We will keep going."

Jules picks up a small frame sitting by her chair and holds it up to the camera. It's a four-by-six frame with an artistically scripted quote on it.

"Minute by minute, hour by hour, day by day. You will keep going" she reads aloud before placing the frame back down. "I've used that advice so many times. It's probably the most relevant piece of advice I've gotten in my life," she admits.

Fourteen

A soft cry, followed by a strangled cough pulls Jules out of the oblivion she's been in. Opening her eyes, she's greeted by pitch black surroundings and the chalky scent and taste of dust. She has a difficult time breathing, and coughs to clear her throat. Something shifts next to her. A hand drifts up her waist.

West.

One arm lies under her, holding her hand while he cradles her back to his chest. His free arm shifts to her cheek and he mumbles incoherently as he tugs at her top. When the house first came down, West ordered her to cover her face with her shirt so they wouldn't breathe in the dust. Her cheerleading top was too short and tight to pull up from the bottom, so she had to duck her face down and pull the neckline up. It barely covers her nose, and even then it's difficult to keep up. She takes small breaths now, careful not to stir the rubble around her face too much.

She moans softly as she shifts. They only have a few inches to maneuver in under the collapsed rubble of the Victorian farmhouse where they sought refuge.

"Jules?" West's voice is raspy and worried.

"Hmmm?" He's a furnace at her back, spooning her. She wants to turn toward him. She needs to.

"You passed out. You okay? Are you in pain?"

"Passed . . . out?" she wheezes with a small cough. She thinks for a moment. She feels alright, and other than the burn in her lungs from her harsh breathing, she doesn't seem to have any injuries. Thanks to West.

"How . . . you?" She struggles to speak as she wiggles a little more, testing her surroundings. Although her free hand touches sheetrock and wood only inches in front of her face, it feels like they're in an open pocket of space. A pocket scarcely big enough for them.

"Don't move. You might hurt yourself or knock something."

"Have . . . to . . ." She pulls her hand from his and with a small groan, pushes herself around. The arm that West has on her waist tugs at her as she twists *toward him, while his other arm stays wrapped under her. She feels his hand press over her head as if he's protecting it from anything that might fall on her.*

"Wow, Buffy—good thing you're so tiny." He chuckles as her face meets his chest and her knee bumps into his leg.

"No fair. The air seems . . . cleaner over here."

"Here." He clutches her hand and brings it to his waist before guiding it up under his shirt. "Hold it to your face and breathe through it," he explains. She notices his voice sounds a little muffled for the first time. He must have it pulled over his face too.

She nods and leans forward to stretch the cotton shirt over her mouth as a breathing mask. Her arm rests against his warm stomach. His hand combs through her hair softly.

"We're gonna be okay."

"How long do you think we've been down here?"

"Not long. They'll look for us, we'll be okay." His free hand restlessly brushes her shoulder, waist, and hip before it weaves under the arm she has in his shirt. He touches her forearm and works his way to find her open fingers holding his shirt to her face. He sighs as he covers her hand with his. Once again, they're holding hands.

Jules wakes in a cold sweat with the smell of dust in her nostrils. Her hand hurts, and she loosens her fist. She was digging her nails into her palm as she slept. Running her thumb over her palm, she can feel the indentations the nails made.

She glances at the clock and is surprised that Jason isn't in her bed. The clock reads two a.m., and she sighs as a tear runs down her cheek. Picking up her cell, she makes an impulsive decision. She locates the number added to her phone barely a few hours ago and types out a text to West. She rationalizes that he probably has his phone on silent and won't get it until the morning, but she doesn't care—she has to tell him.

Jules: My hand misses your hand

She presses 'Send' and flings herself down on her pillow; ashamed for sending it at all. Almost immediately her cell vibrates, except it isn't a return text. He's calling her.

"Hi," she answers softly.

"My hand misses yours more," he offers plainly, no salutations necessary.

"Did I wake you?"

"Nah, I couldn't sleep."

"Me either."

"So, your hand just wanted to text me? Let me know she missed my big, tough grip?" His voice is low, playful. It does crazy things to Jules' stomach.

"My hand's a little whack these days."

He chuckles. "Why's that, Buffy?"

"Two a.m. texts to your hand? C'mon, that's whack."

"First, stop saying 'whack'. You sound like Ruben, and it's strange. Second, you can call me at any hour. You, or your hand."

"Yeah?" Jules asks breathlessly. When did West Rutledge become such a dang charmer? Everything he says is perfect.

"Yeah. I think going through a near-death experience together has earned us the right to be a little needy."

She processes that comment. Is it the experience they went through pulling them toward each other? Maybe it is.

"I think you're right. Thank you."

"Don't thank me. I only said it so I'd feel better about the twenty or so text messages I've typed up but didn't send."

"Twenty? What did they say and why didn't you send them?"

"Jules—"

"Send them now and I'll reply back." She waits for an answer and when he doesn't say anything, she presses on. "Come on. We're both up, anyway. You chicken, Spike?"

"I don't think we should go there right now, Jules." He sounds defeated.

"Go where? Come on . . . I'm hanging up and I want a text in one minute, or my hand will be very mad at yours."

She clicks the 'End' button with a smile and waits for his text, feeling giddy, similar to a little girl waiting to open her presents.

West: I can't send you the texts, Jules. It's not right
Jules: I want to know what you were thinking. How can your feelings not be right? They're yours

She smiles as the conversation with her mom hours ago comes to mind. Jules scribbled her mom's words on a piece of paper as soon as she left the room, deciding they would be her motto—*Just keep going.* She stares at her phone and waits for the text from West. She's nearly given up when her phone vibrates. Scooting under her covers, she slides the lock button and reads the first text.

West: I can't stop thinking about you
Jules: Is this one of the 20? I had a dream about you. Well about us and being stuck that night
West: Hey Buffy, don't reply. Just let me send them okay? And yes, that was the first one
West: You're with Stuart. I need to stop thinking about you
West: I can't believe you remembered that kiss. I bribed Karen to pick us. Convinced Wes Gruber to make out with her in exchange for seven minutes with you. I'm not even sorry

Jules laughs; throwing her hand over her mouth as she reads it. He actually bribed Wes and Karen?

West: You smelled like strawberry shampoo. To this day I love the smell of strawberries. It's because of you

West: Why am I texting and saving messages I'm not going to send?

West: I'm crazy, that's why. Whatever. Where was I? Oh—so strawberries and spearmint. You'd eaten a mint. I saw you pop it into your mouth the minute your name was called.

West: Best damn mint I've ever tasted

West: I was going to ask you out . . .

West: My mom died two weeks later, Jules

West: So, yeah. Life changed after that. I dropped out of football. I was stupid. I miss football

West: This is crazy

West: Anyway, Stuart moved to town that same summer and took my spot on the team like it was nothing and you were a goner. I don't care what you say everyone knew you had it bad for him

Jules knows he's right, though she wants to deny it. Stuart moved to town from California and his long, blond surfer hair and style blew away half the girls at school, but he wasn't interested in any of them. He was all about football, and Jules was all about waiting patiently until he changed his mind.

West: Whatever, past is past. Then you sat on that bench Friday night and you were alone for a change. Do you know how often you're alone? Not very. I couldn't help speaking to you

West: Side note: I think it was that sweet little skirt. Whose idea was it to make cheerleading skirts so short? I need to thank them. Your legs look so sexy in that skirt

West: So there you were, alone and sexy, and I spoke. Then . . .
well you know

West: This is like a confessional. Maybe I need to write in a journal
or something

West: Wow. Did I just think about writing in a journal? Grief
counseling 101

West: So I miss you

West: I swear my hand tingles waiting to touch yours again

West: What did you do to me, Buffy? I'm not that guy

One by one as each text appears, Jules alternates between laughter
and tears. She moans and gasps at their content, and each one chisels
away the already thin wall she's erected around her heart where he's
concerned. When they stop coming, she scrolls back and counts.
Twenty. That's all of them, and now she has so many things she wants
to say back, but first things first.

Jules: You're not what guy??

West: The guy who makes a play for someone else's girl

Jules: Oh

Jules: What if I wasn't someone's girl?

There's a pause. Her hands sweat as she grips the phone tightly
and waits for his reply.

West: You'll always be someone's girl

Jules: ?

West: If you're not his girl then you'll be mine!

Jules feels the melting she mentioned to her mom earlier. Oh,
double chocolate chunk brownie goodness, does she feel the *melting*!

Jules: . . .

West: Like I said you'll always be someone's girl. I'd prefer you were mine but I won't steal you from him

Jules: I need time

West: Remember Buffy and Spike?

Jules: Yeah, enemies. At first

West: Exactly

Jules: Never in my life have I read twenty text messages that made me feel the way those do

West: I feel like a girl

West: No offense

Jules: Ha, none taken. West . . .

West: Yeah?

Jules: I miss you too

West: How can we spend four years barely speaking and it doesn't matter but we spend one night in hell and suddenly I want to be with you every moment?

Jules: Stress, ptsd?

West: Uh oh, did they get you into grief counseling too?

Jules: Not yet, but it's been mentioned. My dad was talking to my mom about ptsd. Apparently a lot of people have it right now

West: Do you think that's what this is then? With us?

Jules: ?

West: So we take time then?

Jules: Okay, time

West: I'll see you tomorrow

Jules: You better, I'm going to need you

West: You'll have Stuart

Jules: Yeah, I know and he's great but I figured something out today

West: What's that?

Jules: YOU are my anchor

Her phone vibrates and she answers without a word.

"Are you kidding me, Jules? Do we have to take time? Dump him and be my girl."

"West."

"No, don't you 'West' me. Ask Jeff—he'll tell you. I've been crazy about you for years. I don't want to bide my time anymore." Jules bites her lip at his angry voice. *Stupid, stupid!* she scolds herself. "Damn it, I'm sorry," he apologizes after a brief pause.

"No, don't be sorry. I shouldn't—"

"You just . . . you can't *say* things like that to me." He drags in a deep breath before continuing. "I'm trying to take the high road here, but I don't really owe Stuart jack, so if you press too hard I *will* break."

"I'm sorry," she murmurs, as the tears build again. What is she doing? Stuart doesn't deserve this, and West sure as heck doesn't deserve it, either. *Gah!* she screams mentally, the sudden urge to punch something coursing through her. "Truly, I shouldn't have—"

"Jules, don't apologize for your feelings. You're stressed. Take some time and things will get back to normal."

It sounds as if he's blowing her off, the way he said 'things will get back to normal', so she doesn't reply at all.

"Okay, get some sleep then."

"I'll try. You too."

"Goodnight, Buffy."

"Goodnight, Spike."

Fifteen

"I don't talk about this very often. The day of your—sorry, Tanya's—funeral." Jules thinks back to that day. Her knees were shaking so bad when she got up to speak her eulogy, she thought she might fall on her face as she stepped up the three small steps to the pulpit.

"The church was packed, the same as it was for every funeral I'd been to that week. Your beautiful white casket sat at the front of the church, draped with purple flowers. I remember I didn't know what type they were, but I could smell them from the pulpit. They tickled my nose."

She rubs her nose at the memory, picturing the enlarged portrait Tanya's parents set up on a gold easel by the 'head' of the casket in her mind. It was from the senior portrait session Tanya took a few weeks earlier. By the foot stands two more frames. One is a large picture of Tanya, Katie and herself at a football game; their huge blue and white bows sticking up, spirit paint on their cheeks. The other a picture of her with her entire family, laughing at something off-camera.

Picturing those happy scenes makes it easier for her to forge ahead and tell the story of Tanya's funeral.

"Once upon a time there were three little girls. These little girls walked into their Kindergarten classroom having never met. They walked out of it best friends for life. You see, they all had something in common." Jules pauses, glancing at the casket with a small smile. "They all wore the same purple 'Hello Kitty' backpack slung across their little shoulders." The crowd chuckles lightly as she finishes. "Kindred spirits they were, from day one."

She slides a few inches to the left as Katie speaks.

"Through grade school, these little girls remained the best of friends. They begged their parents to put them in the same dance classes, and they played soccer together—somewhat miserably, I might add." Another wave of soft laughter runs through the crowd at the joke. "They took tumbling and cheerleading. They were inseparable."

"Middle school came and went, and never did a day go by where these best friends didn't speak. They talked about boys, T.V. shows and how to pass Ms. Simpson's Algebra class in the eighth grade. See, there was something special about these girls."

Katie clears her throat and Jules squeezes her hand as she finishes her part of the speech. "It didn't matter what came along, they weren't about to let anything come between them. Tanya was too hardheaded for that. The most formidable of the three, she never backed down from her two best friends. She was the glue that kept them all together when something threatened to tear them apart."

"You see; we are two of those little girls. Me and Katie. Tanya . . ." Jules stops and swallows hard before looking over at Tanya's family and scanning the faces of friends from school; the other cheerleaders from their squad, the football players. Her gaze runs past Ruben and Tommy. Tommy, who was the last one with her that fateful night. Jeff sits next to Tommy, and next to Jeff she locates West. She didn't see him before the funeral started. She knew he was there somewhere because he said he would be, but laying eyes on him . . . well, that makes her close her eyes briefly. When she opens them again, he nods. It's almost imperceptible, a small nod of support, but it's a small shot of the strength only he can provide and she continues. "Tanya was our third. We were more than best friends, we were sisters. And now there are two where there should be three."

"Tanya hated goodbyes," Katie says. "She told us after her grandfather's funeral several years ago that she never wanted to say goodbye again. Said it was too sad; too permanent. So today instead of saying goodbye to our beautiful friend, we'll say, 'Until we meet again'." Katie recites her last line and turns to Jules who finishes.

"Tanya, until we meet again, Katie and I will continue to hold you in our hearts and in our lives. There hasn't been an event in our lives where you weren't one of the first to know, and now you'll always be the first. We both know full well you are the angel on our side in everything we do. How lucky we are to have you watching over us. I'd rather have you here with me—" Tears clog Jules' throat as she finishes, "—but, if we can't have you here, there's no one we'd rather have on our side up there than you. I love you, Tanya. I miss you my best friend, my sister."

Katie and Jules walk around to the casket where they stop. Their backs to the crowd, they both place their hands on Tanya's casket as the song they picked for Tanya turns on in the background. They picked the song 'You'll Be In My Heart' by Phil Collins from the movie *Tarzan*. When they were little, they used to watch it all the time and sing into their little karaoke radios. They wrap their arms around each other's waists and hug for a moment before heading over to Tanya's parents and hugging them, her older sister, and her extended family as their song plays on.

Hand in hand, they walk to their seats in the second pew. Tanya's parents insisted they sit with the family. When she sits she glances two rows back, where her parents sit with Jason snuggled between them. Katie's parents sit next to Jules', and she smiles at them as they take their seats.

The remainder of the service goes quickly. Jules stares at the casket the entire time, her arm linked with Katie's, as they listen to Tanya's childhood Sunday school teacher speak. A final hymn plays, and it's over. The family is escorted out first, with Jules and Katie following behind. As she passes the row with the boys, they all send sad smiles her way. West is on the far end, but he leans forward and catches her eye for one brief moment as she passes.

Near the back of the church she finally locates Stuart and her stomach flips. He is in the first seat of the row, next to his parents. He leans toward his mom and whispers something before he stands. When they are about five pews away, he steps out into the aisle, meeting her and taking her into his arms. Katie walks on as Jules' arms go around Stuart's shoulders. She buries her head in his neck and the dam of tears bursts forth. They aren't loud, unruly sobs, but soft tears flowing down her cheeks.

"You did so good, doll," he whispers into her ear and tightens his arms around her back.

Jules can tell by the noise passing her, the quiet chatter and sniffling, that people are funneling out of the chapel, but she remains pressed against his neck as he edges out of the aisle. There's a graveside burial to head to next, and although she's supposed to ride with her parents, suddenly she wants to stay with Stuart.

"Jules, we need to head out," he prods, pulling her arms from his neck gently. "Can I ride with you?"

She nods and wipes away the tears as she looks beyond his shoulder at his parents. Jules offers Stuart's parents a small wave before they step out into the bright sunlight to find her parents. Stuart's arm rests along her waist; his hand resting on her hip as they stand in a makeshift receiving line. She spots Katie, and together they stand and accept warm words from mourners and several hugs from teachers and coaches as they leave the chapel.

When most of her cheerleading squad walks up, they all step into a group hug. Everyone has red eyes and tissues in their hands, and Jules listens as they speak about one thing or another that stood out to them from the service. Behind her, masculine voices sound and she turns to see Ruben and some of the team talking with Stuart.

Excusing herself, she steps away from her squad, sneaking behind Stuart to where Tommy is standing quietly. His eyes widen when he spots her, and he takes a step forward.

"You did a good job," he offers as she stops before him. "Tanya would have been proud."

Jules huffs. "No, she wouldn't have. She would've threatened to slap us for being all sappy and sentimental."

Tommy chokes on a smile. "You're probably right."

She notices the black cast he wears on his arm. She doesn't know everything that happened Friday, but she knows they ran, and when they realized they couldn't outrun the tornado they threw themselves in a culvert with a large group of other students.

Tornado Safety Tip: If you can't get to safety, lie flat and face—down on low ground, and protect the back of your head with your arms.

They were taught that message in school for years, and it's what they did. It worked for all but two of them; Tanya and another Hillsdale student, a senior named Mike Brown who was well known and well liked as a bit of a class clown type. His was the first funeral she went to, last Tuesday.

Apparently Tommy's arm was broken by some falling debris as they lay there covering their heads. The tornado went by the culvert they'd hidden in, but it was the debris that turned deadly.

"I really liked her, you know," Tommy confesses; his hand rubbing against his cast.

"She liked you too, Tommy."

His gaze goes past her head as he nods. "Hey, my parents are waving for me to go. I'll see you later?" he asks and she agrees, hoping they will be able to talk some more. She stands to the side, behind Stuart and the guys on the football team, when Stuart's mom walks up beside her.

"How are you doing, sweetie? How's your mom and dad?"

"They're okay. Jason is having a hard time, but—" She starts to say, 'We're all alive,' but it sounds so crude in this situation.

"But it's hard. This is going to take a while to recover from. This town will be hurting for a long time."

Jules looks at Stuart's beautiful mother's face, observing the almost bitter look there. She knows it's true. She's learned enough about natural disasters in Social Studies and watched enough newscasts to know how long it takes to get over something of this magnitude. But they will get over it. Texas wasn't built on the backs of yuppies. Texas is full of cowboys, farmers, and indomitable southern people who take pride in their land and their country.

"You ready to go?" Stuart slips an arm around her.

"I suppose we should," she agrees reluctantly, giving his mom a quick hug as they leave to find her car.

Her parents drove separate vehicles so one of them could take Jason home instead of going to the grave site. She sits in the back seat with Stuart, his hand resting on her thigh, as her mom drives slowly to the cemetery, following the funeral procession heading that way. They're silent the entire drive. Stuart acts a little nervous, throwing small smiles at her whenever their eyes meet.

"How was your trip to your grandparents', Stuart?" her mom asks when the silence becomes too much for her.

His hand flexes on her leg before he answers. "It was nice. Obviously, they were so relieved we were safe. You know my mother, too—she's having a hard time dealing with the chaos here."

"Aren't we all?" Jules murmurs more to herself than to them. Her mom nods in agreement; whether it's with Stuart or Jules' own comment, she isn't sure.

"Can you come back to my house after the service?" Stuart asks softly, and it takes Jules a moment to realize he is talking to her.

"There's a reception at the Rivera's house afterwards."

"Oh, well can we go for a bit, then you come back with me?"

"I guess. Mom?"

"Of course you can, hun."

He gives her another nervous smile before turning his gaze out the window. Jules follows suit and watches out the window as they pull into the cemetery and park.

When she steps out of the car Stuart reaches for her hand, and she feigns the need to fix her hair. He stuffs his hands in his pockets instead as she crosses her arms over her chest, rubbing the non-existent chills from her bare arms. She focuses on the backs of the people in front of her, wearing black and crossing the grass to Tanya's final resting place, and she follows them.

Tanya's parents picked a beautiful spot next to a pond, with huge shade trees and benches along a path. As they move closer to the plot, she scans the crowd and the many faces of her friends. She notes arms wrapped around waists and shoulders with hands clasped tightly. People she never knew were friends hold onto each other. Once again, she's struck with the way this event has changed everything.

Out of the corner of her eye, she finds a dark head of messy hair standing in the middle of the crowd. He's taller than most of the students he stands near, which makes him easy to recognize. She never paid much attention to how much he'd grown over the years. He's probably a good three inches taller than Stuart and a head taller, if not more, than the girls around him. She stops walking when she sees him, a strange jolt of jealousy streaming through her as she watches him wrap an arm around the shoulders of the girl next to him. The girl has straight blonde hair with a black, lace-looking headband on, but she can't get a look at her face to know who it is.

"Jules?"

Turning away from West's profile, she answers Stuart. "I need to sit with the family. Mrs. Rivera asked me and Katie to sit there," she remembers; placing her hand on his arm lightly. "Sorry. I should have told you before.

"Oh." He glances around and nods his head toward a group of their friends. "I'll be with the guys, then."

They stand there for a moment and Jules recognizes how truly awkward things seem between them. Trying to cover it, she steps closer and places a light kiss on his cheek before walking toward Tanya's family.

The burial service isn't much different from the other three she's been to this week. A few last words, biblical passages, tearful moments watching family members remove flowers from the large bouquet draped over a gleaming casket. Jules scans the faces of the crowd a few times, although she takes great care to keep from looking directly at West. She finds her mom, who offers her a weak, tearful smile. Stuart, who is standing with Jeff, Ruben, and Tommy, doesn't meets her glances. He seems deep in thought, going from staring at the sky and trees, to bending his head slightly toward the ground.

She knows a moment of surprise as her eyes drift past Carter, Tanya's summer fling. Similar to everyone else around him, he's somber. Beside him stands a younger girl whose eyes are red and puffy. At closer inspection, Jules notices how much she resembles Carter and guesses the girl might be his sister, or some other close family member. Why would he would bring her here? Why did he bother to come at all? She shakes her head, discarding the thoughts immediately. They had a relationship, regardless of how brief it was. She's glad he came to say goodbye.

Once the service is over, she's smothered with hugs by Tanya's large family. She and Katie step up to the casket sitting above the final resting place, where they will lower Tanya's body once the family and mourners have taken their leave. Katie leans in and presses a kiss to the white casket; whispering a few words before plucking a pink flower from the bouquet and stepping back.

"Go ahead, I'm going to take a moment," she whispers when Katie places her hand on Jules' arm to pull her away.

She stands there staring at the casket and the flowers, the place where her beautiful, vibrant best friend will lay forever; and although she wants to fall to the ground and cry, her legs stay strong and no tears come.

When she feels someone step up beside her she doesn't bother looking back; instead she raises her hand and waits for the warm touch she knows will come. The touch she now craves every hour of every day.

"Do you wonder why we lived? Why we were saved, when in all honesty we should have been crushed to death?" she asks, her throat closing on her.

His thumb rubs over hers as he crushes her hand with his. "Every day," West states simply, and she lifts her head to look at his face.

He stares straight ahead, perhaps looking out over the pond, with his shoulders squared and his dark dress shirt stretched over his frame. Once again she's struck by how amazingly gorgeous he is. She can't believe she's been blind to him all these years.

He sighs and moves to pull his hand from hers. "Don't," she insists, noting the panic in her voice.

He doesn't look as she takes a step closer to him and leans into his side. Her head rests against his bicep because he is that much taller than her. He stiffens. She knows she shouldn't seek comfort from him, but she can't seem to stop herself from doing it.

"This is why," he breathes. His voice so soft, she barely hears him over the crowd milling about behind them.

"This is why, what?"

"*This* is why we're alive, Jules." His words are spoken with so much confidence it only takes a moment for her to realize what he means. He is referring to them, together. She sucks in a breath as he raises their entwined hands to his lips and kisses her knuckles.

Sixteen

"Now let me tell you, T—I *knew* I was playing with fire," Jules admits to the camera; pulling out of the story for a moment. "I don't know how to explain it. West Rutledge made me forget everything and everyone the moment he touched my hand."

Shrugging at the screen, she continues on. "So there we were, leaning into each other and holding hands in front of anyone and everyone, when I hear Stuart's voice behind me . . ."

Jules spins around; her hands flying to her hair nervously as she steps away from West.

"I'll see you later," West mumbles before she can speak.

She stands there as Stuart and West pass each other with nothing but a head nod of acknowledgment. The cold shoulder attitude perplexes her. Stuart stops short of Jules and turns halfway around. He watches West walk away and she holds her breath. Did he notice how closely they were standing?

"Your mom is ready when you are."

"Um, okay." She gives Tanya's casket a final touch before allowing Stuart to escort her to the car. Neither of them speak.

The reception is a crowd of family and friends, sitting and standing around eating finger foods and discussing better days. The Rivera's placed mementos from Tanya's life around the house; pictures from school, medals from cheerleading camps. She has flashbacks of her own childhood as she walks around the first floor.

She makes polite conversation with several friends and teachers from school, as exhaustion sets in. After an hour, she wants to head home. Stuart looks about as comfortable as she feels, and gladly agrees to leave when she finds him standing in the backyard chatting with a crowd from school. Her mom is grabbing a ride home with Katie's parents so Jules can have the car, since Stuart rode with them to the house. She throws the keys to Stuart as they make their way to the car.

"Jules? You're leaving?" Katie call behind her.

Her heart gives a small lurch when she spots Katie standing with Jeff and West, of all people. She's been inside since they arrived, and didn't know he was here. She catches him leaning against a porch railing; his body turned half-way toward her, as though he spun around when Katie called her name. His shirt sleeves are rolled up, his tanned arms crossed over his stomach, and his ankles are crossed.

He appears totally comfortable standing there talking with Jeff and she recalls their conversation on the phone last night. He told her she could ask Jeff about his feelings for her. How did she miss their friendship all these years? Has she been that consumed in her own life that she missed so much of what her friends were doing around her?

Katie bounds down the porch steps when Jules doesn't answer her. "You guys are leaving already?" she asks again as she comes up and gives Jules a hug.

"Um, yeah. I'm not feeling well. My head is pounding." Although she speaks to Katie, she maintains eye contact with West. Jeff says something, and West straightens with a shrug.

"I'll call you later, 'kay?"

Katie nods and steps back. "See ya, Stu." She waves and watches them get in the car. As Stuart cranks the engine, Katie holds up her hand and shouts, "Wait!"

"Hold up." Jules taps Stuart's arm and unbuckles her seatbelt, hopping out of the car in time to meet Katie's hug.

"I love you, Jujube." Katie sniffles, squeezing her tightly.

"Awww, I love you too, K."

"How do we get used to this?"

Jules wants to cry again. "I don't know," she admits on a choked breath. "We just do."

They pull back from each other and Katie glances about sheepishly. Jules doesn't care how they look to others. No one knows what they're going through. No one else knows what it's like to be a part of the friendship that she, Katie, and Tanya had.

"You're going to have to get used to me saying I love you a lot." Katie laughs before shoving Jules back toward her car. "Go on, now."

With a small smile, Jules agrees and opens the car door. She's sliding into her seat when something occurs to her and she pauses. Standing halfway in the door with one foot remaining on the ground, she calls after Katie's back.

"Hey, K. Let's do girl's night Tuesday."

Girl's night has been a tradition since middle school. They alternate houses weekly and watch whatever their current guilty pleasure is. The best thing television series' begun doing was start all new summer seasons of shows, thus making girl's nights a year-long event. For some reason, this past summer was more hit-and-miss than usual.

Katie reaches Jeff at the bottom of the steps and hollers back, "Yeah, we should."

"I've been in the mood to watch something old school . . . maybe some Buffy." Jules holds her breath the moment it comes out. Katie is mildly confused, but nods in agreement.

West, on the other hand, isn't confused at all. He turned away from them, Jules suspects to try to be indifferent to her, but the moment she says 'Buffy' his head snaps her way and his signature grin breaks out across his lips. He tips his head her way and she lifts her hand in a small wave. Luckily Katie and Jeff are standing there, and she plays it off as though she's communicating with them.

"Are you ready?" Stuart calls after her.

She slides into her seat with a smile. "Sorry."

"We're here."

The car door slams shut, shocking Jules out of her silent reverie. She comes to and discovers they're parked in the driveway at the Daniels' large house. She was so caught up in her own thoughts, she barely noticed the drive over. They didn't speak a word on the drive over, and she feels guilty for ignoring him. Stuart rounds the vehicle and opens the door for her with a bow.

"Thank you." She forces a smile as she climbs from the car and walks toward the front door.

"Hey." He reaches for her arm, bringing her into his chest and moving his hands up her bare arms, snaking them around her back. "You were awfully quiet on the way here."

"I know, I'm sorry. It's just been a lot to deal with."

"Jules, I'm not complaining." He sighs. "I'm here for you. If you want to talk or whatever, I love you."

She can't speak past the lump in her throat, so she presses a kiss to his neck instead, letting him hold her for a few minutes.

"Come on." She follows him inside.

They find his parents sitting in the kitchen talking. His mother is a typical California girl; long, wavy blonde hair, blue eyes, fit body from all of her personal training sessions. The Daniels have money—lots of it—and Mr. and Mrs. Daniels ooze privilege. They've always been sweet to her and never act snobby, but they've always looked a bit out of place in this small Texas town. Typically, the more affluent families dress in casual, but expensive clothing, but the Daniels seem to find it hard to ever dress down.

Sitting here changed from the funeral, Mr. Daniels looks ready for a country club party, and while Stuart's mom wears a little velvety track suit, she's all blinged out equivalent to one of the Real Wives of O.C.

"There you two are." His mom stands as they walk into the kitchen, her little kitten heels clicking on the tile floor. "Did you get stuck in the detour traffic?"

She walks to the stove and stirs some type of sauce she has simmering in a huge pot. The kitchen smells heavenly, and Jules takes in the salad fixings on the counter and bread sitting on a pan ready to go in the oven.

"You're staying for dinner, aren't you, sweetie?" Mrs. Daniels asks over her shoulder.

"Of course she is," Stuart answers for Jules, and his arm goes around her waist protectively. "Right?"

A wave of dizziness runs through her and she leans into Stuart, lifting her palm to her temple. It's been an exhausting day and she wants nothing more than to lie down, but the look on his face prevents her from saying no.

"Sure, I'd love to stay." She smiles weakly.

Mr. Daniels frowns. "Stuart, why don't you two go relax on the couch until dinner? Jules looks a little pale."

She shakes her head, intending to protest, but Stuart takes immediate action.

"Can I get you something? Is it the concussion?" he asks, concern clearly written across his tan face. "Remember when I had that mild concussion last summer? It made me sick for weeks. I should have thought about that before."

"No, it's alright. Can we go sit though? I'll feel better then."

"I'll bring up some Sprite, sweetie," his mom calls after them, as Stuart guides her upstairs to the media room.

Jules lowers herself onto the huge couch gingerly, folds her legs under her and closes her eyes.

"Why didn't you tell me you felt so bad?" Stuart sits next to her, and her body shifts as his weight causes the couch to sink.

"Come here." He pulls her into the crook of his arm and chest, and she works to keep her heavy eyes open.

"I'm sorry. My head feels so heavy. I'm so tired," she mumbles, before snaking her arm around his waist and snuggling into his warm side.

"Doll, you have a concussion. You need to rest. I should have taken you home."

"No, no—I want to be here with you." She yawns before adding, "I feel like I'm losing you." The words come out in a tired mumble, almost absentmindedly. She probably never would have said them if she wasn't so run down from the funeral. If Stuart thinks anything about what she said, he doesn't allude to it. She feels him shift as he props his feet on the footstool in front of him.

"We'll chill for a bit." He sighs. "Rest, Jules. I'm not going anywhere."

"Tell me about you and Stuart."

Jules shakes her head. Her eyes keep closing on their own, but she wants to keep them open.

"Come on. Don't pass up this golden opportunity to gush about the amazing Stuart Daniels."

"You don't sound like you really want to hear about him."

"Ha." She faces West, lying with her head resting on his bicep. Their heads so close she feels his laughter blow over her. "Of course I do. Tell me."

"Tell you what?" she mumbles, confused.

"About your boyfriend."

"There's nothing to tell."

There's a cracking sound amongst the boards around them. A loud snap sounds and dust falls onto her face.

"Oh no," she moans as debris shifts around them. West's hand comes up and covers her head as they squeeze closer together. Voices yell for them on the other side of the basement, and West answers the frantic shouts.

"We're good!" She hears Lola's cries. What's going on out there?

"Do you love him?"

"What?" Her thoughts are so muddled. It's like she's looking through a glass window covered in dirt, and every time she wipes it clean, another puddle splashes up, covering it with more grime. She has one moment of clarity and splash! Confusion.

"Do you love Stuart? You've been together forever."

"Yeah, I love him." Something nags at her the moment the words leave her lips. "No."

"No?"

"Yeah."

"Jules, I'm used to chicks confusing the hell out of me, but you're winning by a landslide right now." When the wreckage shifts, he tightens his arms and tucks her head under his chin. As he speaks, his breath sweeps across her cheek and tickles her ear.

"I mean that if I'm honest then, yeah, I love him, but I'm not in love with him anymore."

"Since when?"

"I don't know. It's been a while, I think."

"Then why are you still with him?"

"I don't know. He loves me. He's good to me, and like you said, we've been together forever."

"That's stupid."

"Excuse me?" She jerks her head back and knocks into his chin.

"Damn, girl, stay in one spot." His pained grunt fills their little hole.

"Can I punch you when we get out of here?"

"If we get out of here, Buffy, you can do whatever you want to me."

"If?"

"I meant when. Don't get your panties in a bunch."

"Wow, you're a charmer," she mumbles; not sure how their conversation turned from civilized to strange and sarcastic.

"Oh, I'm sorry, cheerleader. Did you want me to be charming?" His voice slips into a low tone, smooth as milk chocolate, and Jules shivers at his breath touching her face again.

"No."

"Jules, sweetie?"

The memory of her conversation with West fades as she hears her name.

"Jules?"

"Hmmm?"

"You've been asleep for three hours."

Jules stretches. While she slept someone placed a blanket across her, and she's burning up now. Kicking her leg out from under it, she pushes herself into a sitting position.

Smoothing her hair back from her face, she checks out Stuart. He's shifted into the corner of the couch, his legs stretched out before him resting on the stool. His arm is wrapped around her shoulder. He's watching the sports network and she smiles because it's such a normal thing to do.

"Oh my word, I'm so sorry. I've been horrible company." She stops herself from commenting on how terrible of a girlfriend she's been as well. Telling West she doesn't love Stuart, whether there's truth to it or not, isn't right. It isn't fair to tell someone else how she feels about her relationship if she isn't able to tell Stuart first.

"Don't apologize, it was nice holding you. I . . . I'm going to miss it."

"Miss it?" Assuming he's referring to next year when he goes away for school, she smiles. "We've got, what, nine or ten months until we need to worry about that."

"Actually." He sits up and shoves the footstool away so he can place his feet on the ground. "Remember I told you I had news?"

"Yeah?"

132

"Turns out that with the tornado, school and football are all screwed up here. The Board doesn't know where Hillsdale students will end up, and regardless of what they decide for the school, the sports program for this year will be pretty washed out."

"How do you know this?"

"My dad talked to several members of the Board. Apparently they are considering re-zoning our school while they rebuild a new one, especially since school hasn't started yet. It would be easier than trying and find one large location for us all."

Jules remembers the conversation with her parents the day before about the same thing. It would make the most sense. She knows right away of several friends who will end up at another school because they live across town, and frowns. Stuart will most likely end up at a different school, too. The Daniels live closer to Robinson High School than they do to Rossview, which is barely outside the city limits from her neighborhood.

"My parents and I met with the coaches at South Houston while we were visiting my grandparents . . . " He trails off, his hand reaching off the back of the couch to skim her shoulder, and she waits for him to explain what he's talking about. She senses his hesitance to continue, so she sits forward and raises her brows as if to say, 'and?'

"Um, they offered me a spot on the team. It's already been cleared by the school system."

"What are you saying, Stuart?"

"Jules, my mom is seriously freaked out by all the damage here. So when we realized I might have to forfeit my senior year of ball, Dad made some calls. We're going to move to Houston and live with my grandparents."

"You, what? Why, what—I don't know where to begin." Rubbing at her temples, Jules watches as he leans forward and tugs a thread from his slacks while she moves to calm herself. "It's our senior year."

"What does that mean anymore? We don't have our school, Jules. I can't play ball here."

"Ball? Seriously? Stuart, you're already locked in at USC. There are other things besides football."

"I know that, but you also know how important this year is for me. I can't sit a whole year out. I need to play, develop, and get ready for college."

He's right, she does know how important it is to him. She grew up with football. She's never given him crap about the time he devotes to it, and she's not about to start now. "You're serious? You're really going to move?"

"It's only three hours away. Nothing has to change with us. I mean, we can make it work. We were going to have to do it next year, anyway."

"Were we?"

Seventeen

"We talked for a while that night. I'm not going to bore you with all of the details, but let's say the future of us—the things we thought were going to happen our senior year? Well, those things became another casualty of the Tyler twister of 2013."

"I left Stuart's house pretty late, my heart heavy, yet hopeful. I took the back roads home that night, my thoughts circling back to West the entire way. He'd been on the fringes of my life all that week, showing up at the house and at funerals, making his presence known at exactly the right time. His touch comforted me whenever I felt as if I was going to lose it."

Tugging on a strand of hair tickling her collarbone, Jules twirls the hair around her finger.

"At Tanya's funeral, I flung myself into Stuart's arms the moment I saw him. I thought it was love that made me so happy to see him, to seek out the comfort he provided when he held me. But as I drove home that night, I realized I was finally ready to admit the truth."

"So I did something crazy . . ."

Jules turns down a dark, winding road two streets before her neighborhood and follows it to the end where it opens up into an empty parking lot. Bringing her mom's car to a stop under a dim street light, she picks up her cell and stares at it. With a deep breath, she locates his number and dials. Her heart pounds as the line rings in her ear. It's nearly eleven o'clock at night, but she can't put this off.

"Buffy?"

His endearing nickname eases her nerves. "Hey."

"Hi."

She fiddles with the keys dangling from the ignition. "I'm sorry, I know it's late. Did I wake you?" she asks after an awkward moment of silence.

His voice is deeper than usual. "No, it's fine. Are you okay?"

Silence fills the air for a moment. "Um, not really," she admits.

West shuffles around on his end of the line. "I'm here, what's up?"

"Can you meet me?" He makes a clucking sound and Jules imagines he's contemplating her question. "You don't have to, it's just—"

"No, of course I can," he says quickly, stopping her. "I can be wherever you want."

"Whitwell Park?"

"Okay, give me ten minutes."

She's able to mumble a quick word of thanks before he hangs up.

Jules climbs out of the car, sits on the trunk and faces the large, wooden play set she played on as a kid. It's quiet here. Woods surround the playground and parking lot; a melody of crickets fills the balmy night air.

She lies back against the rear window while she waits, gazing up at the clear night sky. She closes her eyes, trying to remember those hours missing from her memory on the night of the twister. According to her parents they were trapped for about four hours, and a little over an hour of that was the rescue crews trying to dig them out without bringing the house crushing down on them. Thus far she'd experienced a few flashbacks: West telling her they weren't going to die, her freak-out moment when he joked about dying in the arms of a beautiful woman, the memory of twisting her body around to face him and the feel of his abs under her hand as she used his shirt as a face mask. And the moment she told him she wasn't in love with Stuart. Each memory unlocks a moment with West that draws a mark on her heart permanently.

The rumbling of his motorbike signals his arrival, and Jules rubs her sweaty palms together as she follows the lone headlight moving along the long road. Pulling up next to her car, he kicks his bike stand down and turns off the loud engine.

He's wearing a tight, white tee shirt and ripped jeans, and Jules' mouth goes dry as he removes the helmet from his head, hangs it from the handlebars, and turns his warm eyes her way. He looks both concerned for her and thrilled at the same time.

"Hey," she calls out tentatively, remaining on her trunk for fear her knees will give out if she stands.

"Hey, yourself," he replies with a smile.

Jules pats the trunk next to her as he swings his leg around the bike and stands beside it, looking at her. He glances around the park as though he's hesitant to come closer. "Is everything okay? What's going on?" he asks, unsure of himself. It isn't something she's used to seeing. Any time she's ever noticed West around, he always acts so confident and sure of himself, a quiet loner who does his own thing.

"Can we talk?"

His face wipes clean, as though he's pulled a screen down covering his emotions, as he saunters over to the car and leans against the trunk next to her legs. Two inches to the right and they'd be touching.

"Shoot."

She clears her throat, reminding herself it's high time she figures things out with West Rutledge. "I've been thinking about those hours we were trapped."

"I thought you couldn't remember anything. The concussion, right?"

"Well, yeah, it's like selective memory loss. So, yeah, conveniently enough, I haven't been able to remember all of the horrifying moments after I hit my head." West nods, hooking his thumbs on the edge of his pockets.

"It should all come back, though," she tells him, positive it will.

"Why would you want it to?" he asks.

"Well, why wouldn't I?"

He props his booted foot up behind him on the fender. "It sucked." His voice is filled with emotion and it strikes her how lucky she is that she can't recall the full terror of being trapped. The terror of thinking they could die at any moment.

"I'm sure most of it did," she agrees, her hand reaching out and touching his shoulder lightly. "But not all of it."

He pushes off the car and faces her with a deep sigh. "Look, Jules—"

"Why did you ask me if I was in love with Stuart?" she interrupts.

The question freezes him and he shrugs. Jules simply stares at him, letting him know he isn't off the hook with a raise of her brows.

"I said a lot of things that night to keep you coherent. You obviously don't remember half of what we talked about."

"I keep having memories. They're slowly coming back to me."

"And why is this one important enough for you to call me at eleven at night?"

"I don't know—it was an awkward memory to have." His features clearly show confusion at her cryptic explanation. He lifts his hands in a silent question. "I was at Stuart's house. I woke up in his arms with the memory of myself telling you I didn't really love him."

West raises his arms and takes a step back. "Look, I don't need to know the details surrounding you and Stuart. I should go."

"Oh gosh, no! It wasn't like that!" She slaps her forehead, sliding off the car to stop him. "West?" Her fingers skim his arm and he whirls around, grabbing her by the waist and pulling her against him.

Jules relishes the contact of his hands on her arms as they stand there in silence. Her chest touches his with the rise and fall of each breath they take. She has to crane her neck to look into his face because he is looking over her instead of at her.

"Look at me," she says.

He tips his head and her breathing stops altogether when his stormy, dark eyes meet hers. His eyes speak volumes and she's compelled to lift up on her toes. Her mouth reaches for his as her lids lower, but West's grip tightens and he straightens his arms; resolutely pushing her away.

Holding her at arm's length, his voice is firm but gentle. "No."

Jules swallows back a lump of emotion as a wave of embarrassment washes over her with this, his second rejection. Averting her gaze to the ground, she tries stepping out of his grip. Instead of letting her go, West tugs her back to his body, brushing his index finger across her cheek. Is he going to kiss her in spite of his rejection? He speaks instead.

"One of these days, Jules Blacklin, I'm going to kiss you again, but it's going to be when you're mine—" West moves his thumb from her jaw, tenderly running it across her bottom lip as his gaze locks with hers. "Because when I start kissing these lips, I don't want to know he gets to kiss them after me."

She's sure she's going to melt right into the ground as he watches her. Indecision flashes through his eyes and Jules wishes, not for the first time, that she knew what he's thinking. One moment it's as though he's going to kiss her, and the next he looks mildly furious with her for some unknown reason.

"You know what? I shouldn't have come. You need to go back to your boyfriend, Buffy," he hints, pulling back from her.

It's as if she was involved in a car wreck. Her emotions and feelings are the car, and West—with his words—is some fast-moving object that has thrown itself out into the middle of the street. *What the heck?* West has already taken three steps back to his bike before she can speak again.

"We broke up," she confesses.

He freezes; his back ramrod straight, his arms ending in clenched fists as he stands there not facing her. "Do you want to repeat that?"

She can't help but smile at his tone. "I said we broke up."

He tips his head up, his chin turning ever so slowly as he looks over his shoulder at her. He's skeptical. Even under the dim lights of the parking lot, she can spot the doubt written on his face. "Why?" he turns his body to her fully.

"I told you underneath that house. I don't love him. Not the way he deserves."

"That didn't stop you before," he hints; boredom creeping into his words.

"Really? Do you have to be such a jerk about it?"

"I'm not—"

"Yeah, you are. What's with the tone? The sarcasm?"

"I'm just speaking the truth. I'm not going to sugarcoat everything for you, cheerleader. That's not me."

"I'm not asking you to sugarcoat anything, West. I'm merely asking for a little compassion."

"Oh, that's rich. You want me to have compassion for you? For what?"

"I just broke up with my boyfriend of almost two years."

"And?"

Frustrated by the conversation, she kicks a stone by the car.

"What the hell does this have to do with me, anyway?"

She looks at him standing there with his arms crossed tightly over his chest. He's gearing up for a fight, with his brows knitted together and his mouth tight.

"I did it for you."

"I didn't ask you to dump your boy toy, Buffy."

"First, he wasn't my boy toy, *Spike*." She throws in 'Spike' out of anger at his attitude with her. What's his problem? She thought he'd be happy, but maybe she read all of their conversations wrong. Maybe she's an idiot. As quickly as she thinks it, she brushes the thought aside. Nope, no way is she wrong. She can feel it deep inside—there's something between her and West that is extremely unique. "Second, when I say I did it for you, what I meant was that it's like I told you. I don't love him. I haven't been in love with him for a long time." Her eyes close as she wraps her arms around her stomach and makes her last confession. "I simply didn't know it until you touched me."

What she imagines in her head for this moment is West pulling her into his arms and spouting off something romantic and sweet, or perhaps sarcastically sweet, as is his way. What she doesn't expect is the anger he exhibits when he drawls, "You're joking, right?"

Driven to make him understand, she bridges the gap between them and takes his hand; holding it up between them. She called him tonight solely based on her emotions. She needs to be more honest with him than she's ever been before. "No, I'm not joking. I don't know what this is between us, but I can't stop thinking about you. That's not fair to Stuart."

"Stuart? What about me? You think this is fair to me?" He snaps his hand away and steps back; his anger shocking Jules. "Hey, West, I dumped Captain America for you," he mocks. "What the hell is that?"

"I don't—"

"You can't put that on me."

Jules' mind whirls. "I'm not putting anything on you."

"No?" Sarcasm laces his voice again. "Would you have dumped him if it weren't for me?"

"He's changing schools. Leaving for Houston tomorrow."

West swings his head toward her and Jules retreats from the ice in his eyes. "Oh, I get it. The golden boy is leaving, so why not, right?"

Angry heat rises within her at his words. "Are you mental?"

He growls, running his hand through his disheveled hair. "I'm gonna go."

"You're gonna go?" She backs up, landing against the side of her car, defeated.

West climbs on his bike. His brown eyes watch her thoughtfully, lingering on hers as he puts on his helmet and kicks up the stand. His mouth opens and she waits for him to speak, her heart pounding in her ears. She can't believe he's going to walk away after everything they said to each other over the past few days. The engine roars to life and she straightens, taking a step toward him, a silent plea in her eyes. She knows he can see it. She knows he's aware of what he's doing to her by driving away, and yet he does it anyhow.

Jules stands next to the car, watching his taillight until it disappears down the long, winding road out of the park. The humming of his motorbike the lone noise disturbing the stillness of the night. Weary, Jules sits in the car and rests her forehead on the leather covered steering wheel. She allows herself some self-pity as she thinks about her conversation with Stuart earlier. She's a besotted idiot for calling West here. What was she thinking? She wasn't, obviously. It's so uncharacteristic for her to go out on such a limb. She's the smart one; the thinker. Tanya was the risk taker and Katie is the cheerful ball of energy. Jules, though? She's a planner. Since the twister happened she hasn't planned a thing, and here she is, sitting in her car in a vacant parking lot at midnight, rejected by a guy she never should have thought twice about.

"You're the mental one," she grumbles, smacking the wheel with her palm.

She's barely started the ignition when her phone buzzes. Removing it from her drink holder, she checks her messages.

West: You need to head home. Please

"You've got to be kidding me." Jules searches the parking lot. Is he watching her?

Jules: What do you care? You left me here
West: I care a whole hell of a lot!
Jules: Then what, West? You flipped out on me. No worries, I'm sorry I misunderstood things so badly

Tossing her phone onto the seat next to her, she throws the car into 'Drive'. Her cell buzzes again and she ignores it as she makes her way back to the main highway. When she arrives at the park entrance, she's startled by West, sitting on his bike waiting for her. She closes her eyes for a moment, and leaves the park without looking his way. Drive, she tells herself when her phone buzzes again. A single headlight glows in her rearview mirror and she ignores it as she drives into her own neighborhood; taking the winding turns to her street slowly. West keeps a good distance between them as he follows her home. The roads are empty for a Saturday night, as most people are following the curfew set in place by local law enforcement due to the hazardous conditions existing in the city. She parks in her driveway instead of pulling around to the garage, and waits expectantly for West to come up behind her. Her heart picks up when he slows as he gets closer, but amazingly enough, he passes the house without stopping. At first she thinks he's going to turn around, and she jumps out of the vehicle quickly. It's as though she's in the middle of one, big, cosmic joke as he drives past her standing there and off into the distance.

He followed her home to make sure she got there safely, and he left. She wants to scream. Remembering the missed texts, she dives into the car and checks her phone.

West: Don't be that way. I'm an idiot
West: I'm a jerk . . . I'm so stupid, I'm sorry

Angry now, she speaks aloud, as though he can hear her. "Yes you are. See ya around." Turning her phone off, she heads inside, where she plans on sleeping her confusion and sorrow away for the next few days.

Eighteen

"I holed up in my house for the entire weekend. The stress of the funerals, Stuart's departure, and West's rejection took their toll on me. I must've slept more that weekend than I ever have in my life. My mom began to hover by Sunday afternoon. She didn't ask questions, but she knew there was something going on with me."

Jules thinks back to those first few days after the funerals were over, when she wasn't sure what to do. Tanya was gone and people were already moving on, yet she wasn't sure how to do that . . .

Her first step to normalcy is the girl's night she planned with Katie. Tuesday night Jules carries an armload of drinks, snacks, and chocolate to her room in preparation for Katie's arrival. They've exchanged a handful of text messages since Tanya's funeral, and she's looking forward to having some girl time. So when she opens the front door around seven o'clock to her friend wearing what Tanya used to affectionately call her 'angry face', she's taken aback. Jules moves in for a hug with a confused smile as Katie pushes past her, kicking off her flip flops by the door.

"You wanna tell me what's going on with you?"

"Well, hello to you too," Jules shuts the door behind her.

"Don't play coy with me, Jules. Here or upstairs?" She reminds Jules of an angry sprite, with her blonde hair pulled up into a messy ponytail and a pair of sunglasses perched on her head. Her hands are settled firmly on her hips and her foot taps menacingly.

Katie mad is almost funny. Tanya always made fun of her, because at five feet-one-inch-tall and barely one hundred pounds, she's a tiny ball of muscles and attitude with the high pitched voice of a five-year-old. She's one tough cookie though, and right now Jules is fully in the crosshairs of her ire.

Reluctantly, she motions for Katie to follow her. "Upstairs."

The moment Katie closes Jules' bedroom door behind her, she spins on her in agitation. "Seriously, Jules."

"Seriously, what?"

"You and Stuart break up and I have to hear about it from Jeff? I thought we were best friends."

Jules ignores the fundamental implication questioning their friendship and goes straight to Jeff's name.

"From Jeff? When did he talk to Stuart? It's not like they're best friends."

Katie grabs her hand and tugs her onto the bed. "Don't change the subject, girlfriend. What happened?"

Grabbing a pillow, Jules hugs it to her chest as she crosses her legs and explains everything to Katie.

"It was bound to happen. He's heading to California next year, and I'm staying here. We needed a break."

Katie rolls her eyes. "A lot can happen in nine months. Why now?"

"I—" She stops, thinking back to her conversation with Stuart Saturday night.

Stuart practically jumps off the couch when Jules questions whether they're truly going to try and make things work once he moves to California.

"I'm confused. A week ago we were talking about finally having sex, and now you're questioning us? Why, Jules?"

"Yeah, and a week ago forty-five people were still alive. Things change."

"Things change? What's changed? Can you tell me? Because I still love you."

She bites her lip, standing when Stuart attempts to pull her closer. She walks over to the wall of pictures and trophies that are displayed in the media room. Stuart's years of football glory are laid out unabashedly for all to admire.

"Everything," she whispers; her fingers brushing over the silver plastic head of a football championship trophy. "Everything changed. I love you, Stuart, but I'm not in love with you anymore."

"You're stressed, doll. You need to take some time to rest and let everything sink in. This week has been hell for all of us."

"No." That isn't it and she knows it, although she wishes it was that easy. She wishes she could merely close her eyes and wake up the next morning and everything would continue on the way it always has, but she can't. She can't go back, because every time she closes her eyes, her mind is filled with West Rutledge. Every time she thinks about moving forward, she feels his hand in hers.

"I'm sorry." She faces him and tries to explain. He stands before her, reminding her of a man facing a shooting squad; his face pinched and drawn. "I don't want to wait around for you; for weekend visits, or for football season to end."

"You're mad I'm leaving?" he asks as he steps toward her.

Jules shakes her head, waving a hand to discourage him from coming closer. "Honestly, I'm happy for you. I mean, I'm going to miss you, but no, I'm not mad. I understand it and I'm not sad. What does that say about us, if I'm not sad you're leaving?"

"Jules, don't do this. There's no rush for us to split up. Let's take a break and get situated with our new realities."

"This is the new reality, and I think we should break up." She meets his eyes. "Now."

Stuart crosses his arms, and his stance takes a more aggressive form. His lip curls up as a small laugh of disbelief escapes him.

"This is about West, isn't it?"

She can't cover the guilt on her face fast enough and he shakes his head at her unspoken acknowledgment.

"Really? What, he's your knight in shining armor now?"

"It's not like that."

"Then what is it like? Don't tell me he isn't involved in this decision, Jules. I'm not an idiot. I saw you two at the funeral. This town has eyes, you know that. I also know you went off with him on his bike the other day after the funeral for that sophomore."

"Quinton."

"What?"

"His name, the sophomore, was Quinton. And yes, I did leave with him. He wanted to talk. You wouldn't understand."

"Are you kidding me?" he barks and Jules jumps at his anger. "I totally understand. He's using you. He's taking advantage of you, Jules."

"He isn't using me. I've barely spoken to him in years. We used to be friends, we grew up together, then things happened and it all changed. He saved me the other night. He didn't have to, but he did." She balls her fists thinking about it. "There's something there, Stuart. I'm sorry, but it's not fair for me to be with you when I'm thinking of him."

"West Rutledge? Really? What can he possibly do for you that I can't? He's a loner who skulks around in black and sneers at the world."

"That loner saved my life. You know, the life of the girl you claim to love. Careful, Stuart. Your snob is showing."

Stuart all but growls. Jules sees the anger in his body language, but it's at war with the hurt she can make out in his eyes. She knows his look of pain, and underneath the anger she sees the pain in his crystal blue eyes.

"My snob? Hell yeah, my snob is showing! You're dumping me for a guy who doesn't seem to care about anything. You don't even know him."

"No, you don't know him."

He blows out a deep breath; his head falling back as he looks at the ceiling. He stuffs his hands in his pockets and she watches him silently, knowing her words must hurt.

"Fine. You know what? I'll let you break up with me." Jules gives him a hard look at the 'let you' and he backtracks. "What I mean is, I won't fight you." Leveling his gaze on her, he closes the gap between them.

Jules' head pounds as she forces herself to stand her ground and not slink back out of guilt. Stuart takes her hands and pulls her into his chest; wrapping her arms around his waist. She tips her head up as he speaks.

"I won't fight you because I think you're just confused. I think that whatever happened with the two of you in that house feels important because it was life or death, but you know what? I'm still here. I wish I'd been with you that night. If I hadn't had to meet with Coach, things would have been different. One damn moment. That's all it takes to change our lives, huh?"

"Yeah," she whispers brokenly, resting her forehead against his chest.

"I'm always here for you."

"I know, and maybe I am screwed up, but I need to be fair."

He laughs and hugs her tightly. "I wish I could say I didn't care about fair, but I'll be damned if I'm going to look like an idiot in Houston while you try to figure out what's going on."

"You know I wouldn't do that to you," she insists; pulling back from their embrace.

He drops his arms with a shrug. "Do I? Like I said, people talk."

Jules mentally curses their gossipy small town to hell and back. Whose tongues wagged? She should have known someone would notice her and West's mostly-innocent encounters. Neither of them made any effort to hide their hand-holding at the funerals, and she willingly left on his bike the other day without worrying what anyone thought.

Perfect example? When Mary Anne Hinke wore a red lace bra to a business lunch with a unhappily married man, the whole town heard about it before his wife picked the kids up from school. Her 'friends' learned how to gossip from the best of them—their own mothers.

"Why didn't you ask me about him before now?"

"I trusted you," he admits. "I knew you'd tell me if there was something I needed to know. Of course, I really didn't think I had anything to worry about."

"I'm so sorry, Stuart," she mumbles; trying to keep herself composed.

He walks her through the quiet house without another word. His parents have apparently already retired to their rooms for the evening, and Jules is glad for that. Having to face them will surely make her feel guiltier for dumping their son.

Stuart opens the car door for her and waits as she slides into her seat. She stares out the front windshield as he moves to close her door. He stops and looks at her one last time, his brows pulled together in thought.

"I meant what I said, Jules. I'm here for you, always. Mom and I are leaving to head back to Houston tomorrow afternoon, but you can call me anytime. Maybe you could come and visit in a few weeks, as friends even."

She shrugs. "Yeah, maybe." She doesn't want to tell him that she can't see how they could handle being friends any time soon, but the thought makes her sad. Willingly letting him go, after everything else she's been through this week, hurts.

"So he shut the door and I left. The end."

"Wait!" Katie blurts out, stopping the retelling. "I don't really care what Stuart thinks about it all. Tell me how *you* feel."

"I'm trying." Jules falls to her back and stares at the ceiling. "He was pretty pissed, K. I did a crap thing, didn't I?"

When Katie doesn't immediately answer, Jules wants to crawl under the covers and disappear.

"Are you kidding? You did him a favor! You could have screwed around with West behind his back."

"You know I wouldn't do that."

Katie nudges her leg. "I know. So tell me about West. What happened between you two?" she prods as she grabs a bag of chips from their snack stash.

Jules reminds her friend of the 'Seven Minutes in Heaven' game they played back in seventh grade when she first kissed West, and gives her some information on how he makes her feel. She looks at her best friend, her eager eyes hanging onto every word, and it occurs to her that she doesn't want to share all of the details. Not yet, anyway.

First, There's the way he ran away from her at the park the other night. She hasn't heard from him since, and she certainly isn't going to make the first move. Second, she's confused about everything. She took the past weekend to rest and spend some time with her parents and Jason, all the while trying to keep West out of her mind.

"You know he's always stayed really close with Jeff, right?" Katie offers, once Jules has given every last bit of information she can think of without spilling the more personal details.

"West?"

"Yeah, they never stopped being friends. I was shocked. I mean, it was obvious to me the night of the twister, the way they talked to each other. But I didn't realize how close they were until this week. West showed up at Jeff's house last night."

"He did?" Jules shoots up from her position on the bed, eagerly awaiting more information. Katie smiles knowingly. Busted! Jules reaches for a snack cake, attempting to cover her excitement, while trying to sound interested, but not too interested. "Why was he there?"

The smile lighting Katie's face tells Jules isn't buying her casual question. Katie reminds her of a little kid ready to spill a super-special secret, and Jules' pulse quickens; knowing she's about to hear something good.

"Well, Jeff and I were supposed to watch a movie. We'd settled down when Mr. Dark and Moody walked into the house without so much as a knock." Jules laughs at Katie's spot-on description of West she frowns.

"Of course the Parker's weren't home, and apparently West knew they were out, but c'mon! Most people would knock. What if we'd been in the middle of something . . . you know, private?"

"Whatever could you mean?" Jules teases, eyeing her friend suspiciously. Have Katie and Jeff slept together yet? She knows Katie isn't against it, and they've been close many times before, but they always seemed to break up before they did the deed.

Katie's pale skin blushes ten shades of red and Jules is pretty sure her answer is in those crimson cheeks.

"Anyway, West comes stomping into the house, blurting out as loud as he can how screwed he is. He must not have noticed me, because as soon as he did he cussed like a sailor and almost left before Jeff tore him a new one and told him to stay."

Curious, Jules takes the bait. "What was wrong with him?"

"Technically—" Katie eyes shift from left to right as she lifts her shoulders furtively, pretending she's dispensing classified information. "I have no idea, because I politely excused myself from the room."

"You what?" Jules gasps. Katie raises a hand, shushing her.

"But in reality, I excused myself and stood in the hallway so I could hear every last word."

"You're terrible!" She hits Katie upside the head with a throw pillow. "Now tell me every last detail," she laughs with a conspiratorial grin.

"He was so pissed off he was almost incoherent at first. Kept talking about some spoiled little cheerleader who he couldn't stop thinking about. Jeff had to talk him down from his psycho rant."

"Spoiled cheerleader!"

"Imagine my surprise when I realized he was talking about you." Katie laughs at Jules' glare.

"So I'm standing there listening to Jeff ask him what's up his butt, when he says 'They broke up'. Of course my curious mind went into overdrive, especially when Jeff seemed so shocked by that little revelation."

Katie's face takes on a serious look before she continues. "You know what he said next? Jeff, that is."

"What?"

"I quote, 'It's what you've been waiting for, man'. I started having heart palpitations. Imagine, West Rutledge, Man of Mystery, pining after some girl—a cheerleader, no less. At that point I still didn't realize it was you. For all I knew, it was some chick from another school, but what he said next gave you away. I peeked around the corner from my hiding space and saw West with his elbows resting on his knees and his head in his hands, and in the most broken voice I've ever heard come out of a guy's mouth he said, 'She dumped him for me. Mr. Football, for me. What if I screw it up?'" Katie's hand touches Jules' knee. "Jules, I don't know what all went on between you two, and I sure as hell know you're leaving out a lot of your story, but that boy is in love with you, and it sounds like he has been for a long time."

"Why would you say that?" she asks. She pictures West sitting in Jeff's house, confiding in his friend, and her hands begin shaking. Guys don't normally confide in each other about these things, do they?

"Jeff, for one thing. I had him fill me in on a few things after West left. Before that though, West went on to tell him he'd been a jerk to you. Something about you calling to let him know you and Stuart broke up, and he got pissed at you. From what I could gather, he's totally freaked out about screwing up. I don't know what his hang-up is there, and Jeff wouldn't say. He did tell me that West has been jonesing after you for a long time—like years. Apparently you're the girl who got away."

"But I didn't," Jules mutters, more to herself than to Katie.

"You didn't?"

"I didn't get away. I need to call him or see him, or—" She jumps up as if her bed is on fire; the bowl of popcorn sitting in her lap overturning and spilling buttery kernels all over her gray comforter.

"Like hell you are!" Jules stops at Katie's serious tone, and she orders her to sit back down. "We're going to have a girl's night tonight, and you're going to let that boy worry over you some more. He doesn't know what he wants any more than you do. Give it time."

"Time? Gah! Stuart said I should give it time and I'll see it's nothing, my parents said we should give it time and things will be normal again, and West and I both said we should take our time—but look at us!"

Katie chuckles. "Yeah, he's busting in houses like a raving lunatic and you, my friend, are keeping secrets about a boy from your best friend."

"Katie," Jules warns.

"I'm not mad at you about it. Okay, I was at first, I won't lie. It hurt to know you didn't tell me, but I get it."

"Do you think I made a mistake?"

"How does West make you feel?"

Jules doesn't hesitate. "Safe. Is that stupid?"

"Of course not. I think we could all use a little 'safe' in our lives right now. Besides, we're seventeen. Maybe it means something and maybe it doesn't, but you don't have to decide your whole future right now."

"Tanya would tell me to get on the phone and call him," Jules says. Silence blankets the room. "Tanya was also a mess at every relationship she ever had, wasn't she?"

Katie smiles a sad smile. "Yeah, I guess she was."

Picking up handfuls of spilled popcorn, Jules thinks about West and the revelations Katie made. She looks at Katie, who's popping the tops off two soda cans, and decides to follow her advice for tonight. Tonight they will have a girl's night, and tomorrow she'll figure out what to do next. By the time Katie leaves, at close to one in the morning, Jules is feeling lighter than she has since the twister happened.

nineteen

Jules wakes in a cold sweat, her heart pounding as she grips her bunched up covers to her chest. Her pillow is soaked from the tears covering her face. The clock on her bedside table reads six fifty-seven in the morning. She sits up, hugging her knees to her chest, and takes deep breaths as her nightmare replays in her mind.

She's standing at the Ice Shack with West, the gravel parking lot is dark and empty.

"Why do you keep following me, Buffy?" his voice slurs as he takes a sip from the silver flask he carries.

"Who's Buffy?"

He opens his mouth to laugh, but instead of laughter the piercing screech of the tornado siren comes out of his lips. Jules turns away from West and suddenly she's standing in an open field. The Ice Shack is gone, and in its place is a blood red sky with a dark funnel cloud cutting its way to her.

"Jules!" a terror-filled voice calls for her and she squints. Off in the distance she sees Tanya running toward her.

"Tanya!"

Jules wants to run for her but she can't move. Looking down, she finds her feet nailed to the ground, her shoes covered in blood. She can only watch as Tanya runs toward her in slow motion. The more she runs, the further away she actually becomes. Tanya releases a terrified scream as the funnel jumps behind her; the winds ripping at her uniform. Jules falls to her knees roughly as the nails disappear.

"Tanya!" she cries, standing awkwardly. She limps and runs, jumping over downed limbs and debris to get to her friend.

"No!" She hears a shout and West appears beside her. He grabs her hand and tugs hard, pulling her away from Tanya's struggling form in the distance. Jules watches her best friend being pulled toward the twister like a vacuum sucking up dirt from the floor. The winds pull her closer and closer to its deadly center.

"I can't lose you! You have to come with me!"

"But what about Tanya?" she shouts over the howling winds.

"You can't save her!"

"I can!" she cries, and he releases his grip when she jerks forward once more.

Running from West, whose shouts echo behind her, she trips and stumbles her way to within arm's width of Tanya. She reaches her hand out, skimming Tanya's fingertips as a forceful gust rips her back. Tanya's arms flail out to the sides, and a foreboding silence fills the air. The wind stops howling, the siren stops blaring, and their eyes meet. Stark terror is written on Tanya's face when she turns back and meets Jules' tear-blurred gaze.

"I don't want to die!" she begs pitifully.

A strange growl sounds as the black funnel inches closer, and Jules sinks to her knees, whispering Tanya's name, as she watches the tornado cover her friend.

"No!" she screams, falling from her knees to her stomach and pounding the earth with her fists in anger.

"Buffy?" West's halts her tantrum when his hand touches her shoulder.

Remembering the twister, she raises up. The sky is now an ominous red and the tornado is gone. She turns to West with a curious glance and falls into his open arms, allowing him to hold her closely as she weeps.

"What's wrong?" He sounds strange to her ears and she sniffles.

"I should have saved her," she confesses into his chest.

His his shoulder shake. "You couldn't save her, Buffy. You can't even save yourself."

"What?"

Did she misunderstand him or mistook his words? She pulls away, looking up and seeing his smile. Her heart stops. West Rutledge is no longer sitting in front of her. Instead, she stares into the face of a vampire; his fangs dripping with saliva as he licks his lips with the tip of his tongue.

"Dinner time." He laughs menacingly, yanking her toward him with a snarling laugh as his fangs tear into her neck. She wakes instantly.

The part about West turning into a vampire would be humorous if it wasn't for the horror of seeing what she imagines were her best friend's final moments in her mind. She reaches out blindly, grabbing her cell phone from her bedside table and pulling up her social media app. Without thinking about what she's doing, she brings up Tanya's page and types a quick 'I miss you' on her profile. She scrolls through post after post of thoughts from different people as her heart rate slows and the tears fade away.

What would Tanya think of half of the comments on her page if she could read them now? Notes from kids she barely knew, coaches, teachers, family members. Jules comes across a simple heart from one person and is surprised it's from Carter. A picture Katie posted from cheer camp is next. Overwhelmed, she clicks to her personal news feed and scans it. Stuart posted about his new school the day before: 'Houston is different. But I think it will be good.' She clicks the 'Like' button, but doesn't comment more than that.

As if she's compelled by a gravitational pull, she types in West's name. She smiles as a shot of him with his two older brothers pops up in the search feed. It's an older picture; a winter shot of them all in ski gear. They share the same warm brown eyes and good looks. She stares at the three of them for a long time before she clicks on his name and is brought to his page. They aren't friends. Funny, she thought she was friends with everyone on here. His settings aren't private though, and a few clicks later she's looking at a cover shot of West on a snowboard, flashing his sly grin at whoever took the shot. It seems to be from the same trip as his profile picture, and she's fascinated by this unknown facet of the boy who has filled her dreams, and days, a little too much lately.

Clicking on his photos tab, she scrolls through his pictures being the social media stalking expert she is. She, Katie, and Tanya spent countless hours photo-stalking people through the years. West's pictures are pretty uneventful, though. There are pictures of his brothers, football games at A&M, some shots of motorcycles, and a few girls making duck faces in selfies with him. He's tagged in more shots, parties, candid school shots, and friendly girl pics. None of the girls look to be a girlfriend. In fact, she can't recall seeing him with a girl since Carley in tenth grade. Exiting the photos tab, she reads his last status.

"I wish I could hold your hand right now."

Her breath lodges in her throat as she reads those nine words typed at midnight, on Thursday. It was probably less than thirty minutes after their argument at Whitwell Park. The post has several likes—all from girls, naturally—and one witty comment by a guy she doesn't know which reads, 'Door's unlocked, come over.' She giggles all the while feeling the need to cry.

What's up with you, West Rutledge?

Early morning dawns, and deciding it's pointless to try and sleep, Jules jumps in the shower. She lets the hot water wash over her; renewing her spirit and cleansing away the lingering effects of her nightmare. She pads down to the kitchen where she pours herself a glass of juice and eats some toast. Her dad comes down as she's finishing up and is startled to find her there.

"You're up early, pumpkin." He smiles, pressing a kiss to the top of her head.

"I couldn't sleep."

"I can understand that. Your mom is in with Jase again." His eyes are sad as he pours a travel mug of coffee. Jason switched to sleeping with her parents every night after the first few he spent with her. This week, in preparation of going back to school next week her mom is trying to make him sleep in his own bed, but he keeps waking up and begging one of them to sleep with him by the middle of the night. Jules has no idea how to help him overcome his fear. She's having dreams about vampires and Tanya, so she isn't exactly an expert on the matter, herself.

She watches her dad putter around the kitchen; making his coffee, putting leftovers in a lunch box, and grabbing his customary energy bar for breakfast.

"Hey dad?" she asks. "How are things at work?"

"How do you mean?"

"I was wondering what things are like now. In town, with people . . . never mind." She shrugs and he sighs.

"Oh honey, you can ask, you know. Things are different. There's a part of me that feels so guilty every day when I go to the office because I pass so many places ruined by the twister. I have to work, though. The whole town has to get back to normal."

"How?" She stands as she asks the one question she hopes he can give an answer to. "How do we get back to normal when normal is gone, Daddy?"

"You find a new normal, Jules."

But I don't want to. Ten minutes later, she hugs her dad goodbye and plops down on the couch in the living room. She stares out the window at the bright blue sky and debates about what to do for the day. She has four days left before school will finally start. It was delayed for two weeks due to the state of emergency declared in Tyler, but she finally received her reassignment, Rossview High, the day before. She certainly isn't looking forward to the complete awkwardness she sure it's going to be.

It isn't yet eight in the morning when she grabs her bike and heads outside. She considers taking her mom's car, but doesn't want to wake her, and she doesn't know if she'll need it this morning or not. Tyler is small and the town center is exactly that—in the center—with everything a few blocks away in each direction. A few blocks from her neighborhood, Jules rides into mid-town where her father's office is located, along with many other professional office buildings. This area was untouched by the storm, for the most part. The most damage was done on the main drag strip running through the town center. Hillsdale is located directly north on Main Street, and the tornado touched down somewhere due north of that. It ran south along Main Street and demolished the school, shopping centers, and restaurants along its straight path until it hit the furthest southern tip of Tyler, the Ice Shack, and Grier house. After hitting the field, it jumped over county lines into Rossview, where it hit a small farm and fizzled out within a mile of Tyler.

As Jules pedals her way around the crews working throughout town, she thinks about Stuart's mom. She kept complaining about the damage throughout town; the devastation that made it impossible to go anywhere without seeing a reminder of that night. Where Mrs. Daniels couldn't stand to face it and wanted to get away, Jules has an overwhelming need to stop and help. She doesn't want to ignore what's happened to her town. She wants to help. When she comes across a familiar black sports car pulled up outside of a ladies boutique off Kenilsworth Street, she stops. *Gail's* is one of her mom's favorite little shops in Tyler. Normally, it carries high-end clothing as well as custom handmade jewelry and accessories. Now, it's a wreck. The glass front is smashed out and covered by plywood. The doors are propped open, rock music carries into the street from inside the store. A shirtless male strides out the door carrying a large metal trashcan. She watches as he dumps the contents into a dumpster on the sidewalk. He lowers the can to the ground, swiping his forearm across his forehead, and glances up as if he senses her standing there, straddling her bike, a few feet away.

"I thought that was your car," Jules calls when it doesn't appear as though he's going to speak.

"Um, yeah. Hey," Carter replies hesitantly, looking around as though he expects someone to show up. "Out for a leisurely ride?"

Jules looks down at her bicycle and smiles. "I was. What are you doing here?"

He steps toward her hesitantly and she notices a small limp. "Gail's my mom. I'm helping her out."

"Oh." She never knew his mother owned this shop. How does she not know this? She hasn't been in the store with her mom in years, but something flits through her mind; a forgotten memory of a framed picture behind the cash register. A boy and girl about her age. "She keeps a picture of you and your sister on her counter, doesn't she? I remember seeing it when I was in with my mom before. I didn't know that was you."

"Why would you?" he shrugs.

"True." She sighs.

"She doesn't advertise me as her son. She worries about business."

"The rivalry?"

"Yeah."

The rivalry between Rossview and Hillsdale has gone on for years. Friday night fights is the tip of the iceberg in the hell the players wreak on each other, and the towns.

"Speaking of," he drawls, looking around again. "Where's your posse?"

"I don't have a posse."

"No? I heard about Daniels moving to Houston. A little mess scared them away, huh?"

Jules fumbles to answer this. She should stick up for Stuart and his parents, yet she can't deny she feels the same way about them. Instead of replying, she tips her head and climbs back onto the seat of her bike, getting ready to push off. Carter's face screws into a reluctant smile as he picks up the trash can again.

"Hey," he calls as she starts to pedal away. Jules checks over her shoulder and turns her bike in a loop, stopping back closer in front of him. "I'm sorry about Tanya. She talked about you and Katie a lot."

"I . . . um, thanks." She blinks back tears. "Do you need some help? Cleaning up, I mean?"

"You don't want to help with this."

Her mind made up, she steps off her bike. "Sure I do." Carter eyes her skeptically and she explains. "This is my town. I want to do something to help."

"Even if we're rivals?"

She laughs and props her bike on its kickstand. "Not anymore. Starting Monday, I'm a Rossview Knight, too."

"Really?"

"Yeah, really," she deadpans. She follows him into the now-empty store and surveys the space. All the merchandise and shelving has been removed, and there are some cans of paint lying in the corner.

"So, cheerleader," he drawls, and Jules is immediately reminded of West. "Can you paint?"

"Who do you think makes all those amazing spirit banners around the field and school on game days? We're smarter than you think, water boy."

He releases a low whistle, shaking his head. "Low blow, princess." Jules bursts into laughing and Carter joins in.

Twenty

Jules and Carter work for two hours lugging the last of the construction debris and broken glass to the dumpster before they finally pop open the cans of vibrant green paint.

Most of the time they work in silence; his speed metal playlist filling the air between them. She can't help but study him whenever he isn't looking her way...his tan skin, nearly black hair, and light eyes. His body is in prime shape. Texas sure knows how to grow 'em.

Once they're ready to paint, Carter throws her a water bottle and finally turns his music down a notch.

"So the good thing is, we don't have to worry about splattering paint on the floor here." He taps his toe at the concrete floor below their feet, explaining how the carpet installers will be there in the next few days to finish it off. "You can quit now if you'd want."

"No way. This is the part I've been waiting for," she teases as she takes a roller from his hand and covers it in paint.

"You're not going to start cheering, are you?"

"No, wise guy."

Jules lifts the roller, covering the wall in the cheerful green. It's funny how at ease she is helping Carter out. They barely say a word once they start painting, and yet she doesn't mind. It's nice having something to do and not needing to fill it with idle chat.

"Where's your mom? Why are you here all by yourself today, anyway?" Jules asks as she dips the roller in more paint.

"She'll be here soon. She's meeting with her insurance company again. So much red tape with all of this crap."

"How so?"

"Hell, I don't know. That's just what she says," he shrugs.

"Sorry it took so long, sweetie," a woman's voice calls from the entrance. "I grabbed you lunch, though."

"Speak of the devil," Carter whistles, giving Jules a side glance before setting his roller to the side. Jules turns mid-roll, as Gail Cooper walks in carrying a deli bag in one hand and a handful of painting supplies in the other. Mrs. Cooper has always struck her as refined when she's seen her around town. She's several inches taller than Jules, with board-straight black hair she typically wears pulled up in a simple chignon.

"Oh!" She stops and eyes Jules, almost warily. "I didn't know you enlisted help."

"Mom, this is Jules—"

"Blacklin. I know, honey," she interrupts with a smile. She sets the supplies on the floor and the food on a table sitting in the corner. "This color looks fabulous. You're more than halfway done."

"Thanks to my assistant here," Carter acknowledges. Jules' face flushes.

"I told him cheerleaders were masters at painting, but he didn't believe me," she teases lightly.

"Yes, well thank you for helping. Why don't the two of you take a break, and I'll earn my keep for a while? I bought Carter more than enough for two, so he can share."

Jules is prepared to decline the offer, but Carter reaches around her and plucks the roller from her hands. "Come on. The warden says break, we break."

He throws her two unopened water bottles, grabs the deli bag and motions for her to follow him out the store front. The sound of buzz saws and hammering fills the town center as clean-up and restoration is underway. Crossing the street, Carter lowers himself to the curb next to his parked car.

Kenilsworth is a side street branching off of Main Street, where most of the construction is taking place. Gail's is two buildings down from Main, so when they cross over to eat, Jules is pleased to see they're at the corner of Main and Kenilsworth where she can watch all the action. Currently Main is closed from three blocks north of Kenilsworth and one block south. The street is filled with dumpsters, power trucks and tree removal crews. Although the street is a mess, Jules' heavy heart lifts at all of the volunteers lending a hand.

"You know my mom was lucky. Her building is actually standing. Have you gone up Main? Once you get past Queens, the stores are just gone." Carter unwraps a sub sandwich and hands Jules one half. "Here."

She squints up the street, wishing she could see past the large dump trucks as she reaches over and takes the sandwich. "You don't have to feed me, you know."

"You didn't have to help me."

"I know."

"So why did you?"

Jules stretches her legs into the street in front of her, scratching at the specks of green paint splattered across her shins. She studies Carter from the corner of her eye and instantly sees why Tanya was interested in him. He's Abercrombie & Fitch-poster-boy fine.

"Did the paint fumes get to you?" He grins.

"What? Oh, no. Sorry. I was just—"

"You were checking me out."

"No," she cries, flustered beyond belief. "I mean, yeah, actually I was, but it's not what you think. I'm not interested in you or anything."

He nods. "I know."

"I just . . . I was thinking of Tanya and how I could see why she liked you." She stops when his words finally register in her head. "What do you mean 'you know'?"

He laughs. Placing his sandwich in his lap, he takes a long swig of his water. "I've got eyes, Jules. I saw you with Rutledge at the funeral last week." She forms a silent 'Oh' as Carter wags his brows. "You've got balls girl, hanging onto him with your golden boy across the way. I can't imagine Daniels took that well."

Her cheeks flush. Stuart was right. She and West weren't in their own little bubble at that moment, and people definitely took notice.

"Daniels is a prick, anyway. You should dump him and go out with West. It's obvious there's a thing between you two."

"Wow, pry much?"

"Sorry, I just call it like I see it," he offers. He stuffs the last bite of his sandwich into his mouth with a grin. She's barely taken two small bites of her half. Boys!

"Of course you think Stuart's a prick. He killed Rossview on the field three years in a row. Are you speaking from jealousy or from personal experience with him?"

Carter squints. Jules struck a nerve with the football jab. He stands abruptly and balls up his trash.

"Look, I don't really care who you date. I barely know you, but Tanya loved you so I was trying to be nice. Like I said, I like West, and I saw you two the other day. I should get back in there. Thanks for helping, Jules."

Jump back! How the hell did this escalate so quickly? Her jaw drops as he crosses the street leaving her on the curb. She's putting together an apology when a motorbike turns the corner and comes to an abrupt stop in front of Carter. Jules would know that bike anywhere. She fights the urge to crawl behind Carter's car and hide from West as he lifts the visor on his helmet.

"Hey man," Carter calls when West cuts his motor.

West replies in an indistinguishable low voice, looking over his shoulder as Carter points to his mom's shop.

She forces herself to her feet, the paper sack in her hand crackling loudly as she wads it up. West leans to the side, his brown eyes peering around Carter at the sound. His brows lift as his head snaps toward Carter, and his fingers unsnap the strap across his chin. Removing his helmet, West slides off his bike in one fluid movement. Setting the helmet on his seat, he steps around his bike, leaving it sitting in the middle of the street.

Carter steps back, raising his arms in defense, when West strides toward him. "Whoa, man, she was just helping me paint the shop. Nothing else."

She can barely see West with Carter's body blocking him from her view, but she can feel the tension rolling off of him. When he finally speaks to Carter, relief runs through her.

"Excuse me." Two words, spoken deliberately and specifically, are all he has to say to make Carter jump to the side, and suddenly Jules is face to face with an unreadable West Rutledge.

Ten feet separates them. They stare each other down for a beat before his lips twitch; the left side pulling up in a small, crooked smile.

He lifts his hands, whispering 'Buffy', and she notes the spark in his golden brown eyes as his long legs take three strides, closing the gap between them. Jules stumbles back, bumping into Carter's car. Her heart pounds so hard she's positive he can hear it. West's determination is obvious, although his intent is questionable. His chest bumps into hers, causing a shiver to run through her, warming her to the core, even as her skin breaks into goose bumps.

She opens her mouth to reply, but West swoops in, silencing her with his lips. His hands move to the back of her head as his fingers slide into the hair at the base of her skull; holding her in place as his warm mouth claims hers.

She surrenders to the hard kiss immediately, allowing him to invade her mouth with zero protest on her part. His large body pushes into hers, pressing her against Carter's car; the grill digging into her bare thighs. The whole world goes silent as he kisses her, the feeling of his fingers rubbing the back of her neck calming her senses. *Wow, I could stay lost in him all day.* He makes a small groaning sound in his throat and finally lifts his mouth from hers. She nearly moans at the loss of his lips on hers, as he kisses her cheek twice, grazing the side of her mouth.

"I'm not screwing this up again." He plants one more swift kiss on her lips, before lowering his arms from her head to encircle her waist; pressing against her lower back. "I'll be damned if I let another guy step in and get a chance with you before I do." He all but growls the words as his eyes meet hers.

"I . . ." she starts, but he covers her mouth again.

"Shut up and kiss me, Buffy," he orders softly into her mouth.

The lunch sack and water bottle slip from her fingers as she draws him to her, her hands fisting in the shirt at his back as she kisses him.

Carter coughs behind them. "Well I'll leave you two alone, I guess. Be careful of the paint job, Rutledge," he heckles.

Neither of them reply as they continue to explore each other's mouths, this time a bit softer and slower. West's thumb rubs along her jaw as his teeth graze her bottom lip. He tugs it into his mouth gently and she sighs contentedly. His fingers skim the skin at her waist, causing her muscles to twitch.

"Why the hell are you hanging out with *Carter Cooper*?" he grumbles when he drags himself away from her mouth with some reluctance.

"You're going to let me speak now?" she asks; releasing her fingers from his shirt and flexing them.

"Actually—" He grins and tilts his mouth toward hers again; his eyes on fire.

She laughs into his mouth when his lips touch hers and punches his side lightly. "I need air," she gasps playfully.

Pressing her fingers to her tingling lips, she attempts to control her ragged breathing. They are standing in broad daylight making out for everyone to see. She feels the heat of a blush surge up her neck and into her cheeks.

Sidestepping West, she regards him with uncertainty. "What was that?" She asks, meaning the surprise kiss.

He tugs on the bottom of her shirt as she slips from his arms, his face openly questioning her movement.

"How come you're hanging out with Carter?" he counters.

She laughs with a shake of her head. "I don't think so, bud. I asked you first."

She bends down picking up the dropped lunch sack and reigning in the emotions he awakened with his kiss as she awaits his reply.

"It was just a kiss."

"You kiss all the girls you know like that?" He smirks and her ire grows. "Nice way to accost a girl on the street, Rutledge," she scoffs, brusquely knocking into his side.

He draws her in by the waist as she attempts to pass, pressing her back against his chest, and she stiffens at the contact. West leans over her, his lips moving to her ear, and her nostrils fill with his uniquely male scent. It's an interesting mixture of gasoline and spearmint that makes her stomach flip.

His lips graze her ear as lightly as a butterfly kiss as he whispers, "You didn't seem to complain, Buffy."

Her knees go weak with his hot breath against her sensitive skin, and another shiver races up her spine as his hand drops from her waist. Shaking off the chills, she rounds on him—a snarky comment ready on her lips. However, as soon as her eyes take in his knowing grin, the words are silenced. She can't whip up enough strength to tell him he is mistaken, because of course, he isn't.

After a face-off, he repeats his earlier question. "You and Carter?"

"I was riding by and saw him. Asked if I could help."

"You're friends?"

"No." She's quick to point it out, although she feels as though they are actually friends now. Maybe? West's face scrunches up in bewilderment, and feeling as if more of an explanation is due, she continues. "Um, he went out with Tanya this summer. I guess, I don't know. When I saw him I just felt like I needed to stop and speak to him."

Understanding crosses his features, smoothing out his face, as his shoulders relax and his stance becomes more casual. Jules waits for him to say something more, but he merely stands there watching her; his brown eyes scanning from head to toe and back.

"Well, um, thanks for that kiss, I guess," she finally babbles. She skirts past him, crossing the street and throwing her trash into the dumpster. The entire time, she feels the heat of his eyes boring into her backside as he watches her walk away. She slows, her head locked in an internal debate as to whether she should go back into Gail's and help Carter finish painting, grab her bike and flee, or beg West to kiss her again.

She's never craved a kiss the way she craving another one from him, and it scares the hell out of her. When she first started dating Stuart she longed for his kisses. There's no denying that he was able to get her excited and ignite passion within her, but West? West's kiss doesn't merely ignite passion, it ignites *life*—a burning, crazy fire and zest for living that she's never felt before. Not ever.

"Damn you!" she hisses, spinning on her toes and stomping back to his side. "What the hell was that kiss for? Why did you walk away from me last week? You brushed me off after I opened up to you."

As she stomps and waves her hands in his face, a smile slowly grows across his lips. His eyes twinkle and Jules' anger boils over.

"Don't you dare kiss me ever again," she blurts, pushing against his chest. West laughs and catches her hands before she can pull them away. "You arrogant jacka—"

The slanderous name is swallowed by his lips as he fists a handful of hair and pulls her to his mouth. She wants to scream at him, yet the contact of his lips soothes her and she wilts, turning into a gentle flower in the Texas heat.

He pulls his mouth away from hers enough to speak; their foreheads barely touching. "I already established I was a major jerk the other night when I sent you texts saying I'm sorry, so let's not waste time repeating arguments or lying to each other. I'm a jerk, and you *sure* as hell want me to kiss you again."

"Am I wrong?" he asks when she stares into his eyes moodily.

"No."

"Oh, you wound me," he confesses, nudging her nose with his. "I was hoping you would at least disagree with the part about me being a jerk."

She throws her head back with a small shout of laughter. "Sorry to disappoint you, but you *are* a massive jerk," she points out, and West frowns. "But—"

"I like butts," he winks.

Jules works hard to suppress the smile he brings on. Her free hand cups his face as she continues in a serious tone, "But you were right. I *do* want to kiss you, West Rutledge. Why fight it anymore?"

"So there's really nothing stopping us anymore?"

She shakes her head as his mouth works its way along her jaw.

"Then can you come with me now?"

"Where?" Jules is drugged by him. One hand holds her wrist to his chest from where she pushed him, while the other drops her right hand and massages the base of her skull; lulling her into a relaxed state.

"Does it matter?"

"No."

And it doesn't. She would go anywhere with this boy. She knows it right then and there. She takes his outstretched hand and follows him to his bike without looking back.

Twenty-One

Jules isn't surprised when West turns into the gravel trail that runs behind South Berry Farm. The acres and acres of cornstalks stand much as they did the week before when they were there, and Jules allows him to pull her along a trail deep into the crops before they fall to the ground.

"It's so peaceful here." She lifts her face up to the azure sky.

West props himself up on his elbow and stares at Jules' profile, making her squirm in discomfort. His stare is so piercing, it's as if he's trying to wiggle into her thoughts; to look past the outside shell and into the real her.

She raises her brows as he leans closer.

"Can I kiss you now?"

"Shouldn't we talk?"

"I'd rather kiss you first. We can talk later," he hints; his free hand curving over her stomach and rolling her to her side.

She not able to protest once his warm lips touch hers again.

"Talk is overrated, I suppose." She rolls into his body, returning his kisses with one-hundred percent commitment.

West runs his hand over her backside, which makes Jules giggle into his mouth.

"What?" he whispers against her lips. His fingers grip the skin where her leg curves into her bottom. Stuart touched her intimately throughout their relationship, but having West do it makes her giddy.

"Your hand is on my, um, nether region."

"Oh, uh, sorry?" He coughs and moves his hand. She sits up with a laugh and scrapes her hair back from her face.

"I wasn't complaining," she admits as she sits lotus-style and he sits up next to her. "It's just weird."

"Weird, how?"

He's obviously wary of what she's trying to say, so she considers her reply carefully. "It's you and me."

"Could you possibly be a little more vague?"

She rubs her hands together and bites her lip before taking a look around. She's nervous all of a sudden sitting here with him.

"Jules? You can tell me anything," he encourages; reaching across and wrapping her hand in his.

Inhaling deeply, she lets her thoughts out—the ones that built up throughout the week as her anger with his behavior Thursday night simmered.

"You're Spike and I'm Buffy, right? Like fire and gasoline. The rebel boy who walked away from everything and the cheerleader who dated the golden boy. We are so cliché."

West snorts derisively. "More cliché than the head cheerleader dating the quarterback?" Jules' mouth snaps closed. "What's your point? So we're cliché. I can't douse this fire any more than you can."

Jules' heart races at the way he describes the link between them as 'fire'. It's exactly how she feels. "Fire?" she repeats.

West's brows knit together, as though he's embarrassed he spoke the words, before he nods. "Yeah," his lips curve into a smirk. "I want to be near you all the time. Like, freaking stalk-your-house-and-stand-outside-your-window, near you."

A giggle escapes her lips as she sidles up against his side, her hip pressing into his thigh. Touching her head to his shoulder, she sighs.

"I get it, West, except for the crazy stalker issues. I meant it when I said that everything changed the moment you touched my hand."

"It changed for me, too. I need you." He places a quick peck on the top of her head.

"Then why did you freak out on me at the park?"

"Because I suck?"

"Not good enough. After the twenty texts you sent me, the conversations we had, the moments we shared last week during the funerals, you walked away from me Thursday night when I was baring my soul to you." She can't hide the hurt in her voice.

"Come here," he whispers, pulling her across his leg and situating her between them. Her back presses against his chest as his arms wrap around her tightly.

"You told me you dumped Stuart Daniels because of me. I know I may act like I don't care about much in this world, but I do. It freaked me out. I wanted you to be sure of what you'd done. I don't want to screw this up. You're too perfect for me to screw things up."

"I'm hardly perfect, and Stuart is far from being the golden boy everyone thinks he is."

He buries his face into her neck. "I seriously didn't expect you. I don't like needing things, Jules."

She bites her lip at the soft revelation. *He doesn't like needing things?* She stores the information away for now and wraps her arms around his. "Well you're stuck with me now."

"I am, huh?"

"Yep. Remember you said you weren't going to kiss me until I was your girl?" She twists, tilting her face up over her shoulder to meet his smiling eyes. "You've kissed me, West Rutledge. You're done for."

West lowers his head. "I was done for way before that kiss, gorgeous. Way before," he admits, capturing her mouth in another long kiss.

It's long past sundown when Jules walks into her brightly lit house with a permanent smile plastered across her face.

She spent the afternoon with West sitting and talking in the cornfield until the sun set. They talked about the past, old friends and memories from middle school, and ignored the present. Much of the time was spent in silence. It's different from what she's used to. Jules thinks about the hours upon hours she spent with Stuart, and how they were rarely alone or quiet. When they were alone, it was all about making out or sex. Not that they ever did much, but if she'd let him have his way they would have.

They did way more talking than kissing today, but eventually Jules caught West's gaze roving over her. They sat across from one another so they could face each other as they talked. It was helpful to keep some distance so neither of them were tempted to touch the other. She was watching a group of birds hopping around the husks nearby when she West stopped speaking. She turned her attention back to him, catching his eyes focused on her. As if they were his lips touching her, she melted as his eyes lingered on her mouth, moving across her jaw and down her neck. They flickered lower, boldly stopping at her chest before he followed the same trail back to her mouth again, finishing with his hungry gaze locked on hers.

The simple stare made her body so hot she wanted to crawl into his lap and rip his clothes off. She'd inched forward until her hip pressed against his, ready to kiss him, but he surprised her. Grabbing her knees, he'd spun her around to face the same way he was; pushing her shoulders to the ground and shifting her to lay in the crook of his arm and chest while he hovered over her flushed face.

West plastered sweet kisses along her forehead, nose and cheeks while Jules laughed. "Do you need help finding your way?"

He stopped covering her face with his lips, his gaze tender as he tucked her hair behind an ear. "I found it. I'll just keep following you."

Whoa. Her entire body lit up in flames.

"Jules?" her mom shouts from the kitchen, effectively cooling any lingering passion from the evening as she leans against the front door. The fading rumble of West's bike filling the street as he leaves.

"Yeah?" she peeks out the window, watching his taillight fade away in the dusk.

"Where have you been?" Jules jumps at her mom's voice, now behind her. "Was that a motorcycle I heard?"

"Ummm, yeah," she replies timidly, meeting her mom's annoyed face.

Her mom drops her hands to her hips, a dish towel clutched tightly in her fist. "Tell me you weren't on a motorcycle, young lady."

"I wasn't on a motorcycle."

"Yeah, nice try."

"If it helps, I wasn't on it for very long. He gave me a ride home." She gives her sweetest smile, batting her lashes coyly.

"Don't try to charm me, that only works on your father." Her mom rolls her eyes and nods her head toward the back of the house, beckoning Jules to follow. When they step into the kitchen, she goes back to the dishes she was finishing up and Jules pulls out a stool to sit at the counter and watch.

"So I gather you've made a decision, then?" she asks, while drying a large pot.

"I—"

"Jules, sweetie, I know you were with West, and your father filled me in on the scene between you two in the hospital. I was a teen once too, you know. You can't hide that dreamy, over-the-moon face from me."

"Mom," she wails, embarrassed by the accurate assessment of her feelings.

"I also know you and Stuart broke up." She raises her brows, settling a pointed look on Jules.

Since confessing her confusion with West after almost kissing him in the field the day of Quinton's funeral, Jules hasn't filled her parents in on anything that's been going on with her, Stuart, or West. Now she feels guilty for keeping things to herself as her mom studies at her.

"I'm sorry I didn't tell you."

Setting the towel down, her mom reaches across the counter and squeezes Jules' arm lightly. "Honey, I'm not mad at you for keeping me out of the loop, but I'm here if you want to talk. It's been a rough two weeks, and I simply want to know where your head's at."

"Honestly?" Her mom nods with a smile. "I have no idea."

"Boys will do that to you, baby."

Jules smiles at that and tries to explain her position. They've always talked about things, especially boys. With the exception of the steamier details, her mom has always been privy to her dates and moments with Stuart and her few boyfriends before him.

"He was my first kiss, you know."

"Who? Stuart?" Jules wants to laugh at the somewhat astonished face her mom makes.

"No, West. Back in the seventh grade."

"Do tell." She licks her chops resembling a dog drooling after a bone. Her mom loves gossip, and Jules considers refusing to divulge simply to tease her. Instead she explains about the Seven Minutes in Heaven game—one her mom embarrassingly knows quite well, but that's a story for another day.

"Could the boy I wanted almost five years ago be the one?"

"You're young, honey. The right one is most likely years away. And what about Stuart? You thought he was the one." Jules crinkles her nose, signaling that her mom is wrong, and she sees the understanding cross her face. "I guess I'm not as 'in the know' as I once was," she grumbles.

"It's not your fault. This summer changed things with Stuart. It wasn't something either of us saw coming, either. It just kind of happened."

"Are you sure? I know he went to Houston, but that doesn't mean you two can't continue dating each other if you want."

Her parents love Stuart, but Jules wants her mom to know without a doubt that she is certain of them being over. "I'm sure, mom. Stuart and I are going to be friends. It was a nice break-up, as break-ups go, anyway."

"And West?"

She fights to keep the goofy grin from her face when she pictures his chocolaty brown eyes in her head. "I think, maybe . . . well." She babbles, suddenly unsure of how to explain her feelings. It sounds crazy, she knows it does. One day spent together, a few quiet moments holding hands, a life changing experience—she's faced more with West Rutledge in two weeks than she ever has with anyone else.

Her mom's eyes widen and she opens her mouth to speak when Jules' phone rings in her pocket. She pulls out her cell, her heart leaping at the name 'Spike' on the screen.

"Hey, can we finish this later?" She waves her phone and slides off the stool.

Her mom's face falls, but she gives Jules a reassuring smile. "Sure."

Hitting the answer button, she walks out of the kitchen saying 'Hey' as her mom calls out behind her.

"Jules?" Holding the phone away from her ear, she spins around. With a knowing smile, her mom points at her, "Tell him no more motorcycles."

Jules shoots a thumbs up and rushes from the kitchen to her bedroom.

"Hey, sorry about that."

"No more motorcycle, huh?" He laughs deeply through the phone.

"Oh, you heard that?"

"I didn't get you in trouble, did I?"

"Nah. She's cool, but apparently your bike isn't." Jules throws herself across her bed.

"I can live with that, although I like feeling you pressed up against me."

She shivers at his deep suggestive tone. "We'll just have to find other opportunities for me to wrap my arms around you."

"Again, I can live with that."

"Mmm hmmm, I bet you can. So what's up? Didn't you drop me off like, um, twenty minutes ago?"

"Too soon?" he asks innocently, and she chuckles.

"Not at all."

"Good. I'd hate to know you were getting sick of me already. I just wanted to let you know I talked to Carter. He put your bike in the shop since you left it there."

"Oh my gosh, I totally forgot about it! Thank you for checking with him."

"Of course."

"Hey, I don't think I told you I had an amazing day with you."

"Did you let me kiss you? Or did I imagine that?" he asks mildly.

She giggles. "I believe I did."

"So you know what that means then, right?" Jules searches for the right snappy comment, but West doesn't allow her time. "You're my girl, Jules. I told you if you weren't his, you'd be mine. I'm jumping on this train."

"Ha! The Jules Blacklin Express?"

He chokes, "Well it sounded better in my head. I just meant that I let you pass me by once and it took me five years to get another chance. I'm not missing you this time. Can you deal with that?"

"I can more than deal with that. I endorse it and will happily buy you a round trip ticket."

"You're cute, but I don't need one."

"No?"

"Nope, I'm not getting off this time."

Jules bursts out laughing as his words automatically trigger a dirty picture in her head. Tanya's dirty mind has certainly rubbed off on her through the years.

"Dirty girl." West laughs.

"Blame Tanya."

"Shocker."

Her dad raps lightly on the door frame, popping his head through the open crack. He makes a silent hand gesture for her to hang up and go downstairs, and Jules reluctantly agrees.

"Hey West, my parents want me downstairs. Can I call you later?" she asks once her door is closed again.

"Anytime, Buffy."

"Okay, I'll call you soon."

There's a moment when she struggles with saying goodbye. The words 'I love you' want to push from her tongue, and the thought confuses her.

"Jules?" She can't find her voice to answer, but he goes on without it. "I meant what I said. I'm in this, as long as you're interested in being in it with me."

His words settle in her heart and again she bites back an expression of love. *It's too soon. I'm crazy for possibly considering it.*

"I was in it the moment you finally spoke to me. The moment you called me Buffy."

He expels a long breath. Is he as confused as she is by these intense feelings creeping into every pore of her soul?

"Call me as soon as you can."

"'Kay, I will."

"That was the day I learned I could move on. That there was something, someone, who could make me smile and feel alive. You know, you watch towns and peoples' lives destroyed on the news all the time, whether by natural disasters, accidents, house fires or things like that, and you think about it and feel bad for them, but you never realize just how much damage something like that does to a person."

Jules stares at her hands in her lap, eyeing the red scar running down the length of her forearm. "I'm trying to figure it out myself. But that day? That day was a happy one."

Twenty-Two

"Unfortunately for me, happy days didn't necessarily mean happy nights. I ended up with a repeat dream that night. Tanya chasing after me, West begging me to leave her, Katie screaming. I always woke up in a cold sweat; panting as though I'd run a marathon." She shakes her head despairingly at the camera.

"I began to expect them, and that made it a bit easier, but at first it was hard. That's the reason why I was getting a late start the next day. I left Jason to play while I jumped in the shower, and of course you get naked and what happens?" she asks the camera with a nod of her head. "Yep, someone rings the doorbell . . ."

"Jules! There's some guy I don't know at the door!" She hears Jason yelling up the stairs right as she steps out of the shower. "Jules!"

She rushes to her door with a towel wrapped tightly around her chest. "All right! Is it a salesperson? Tell them to go away, but don't open the door!" she warns.

He talks through the door to whoever it is, and she grabs the first thing she can find to throw on before her little brother ends up opening the door to a serial killer.

"He says he's a friend."

"Of course he is," Jules mumbles as she struggles to pull on her yoga pants over half-wet legs.

"It's West!"

She nearly falls on her face as she trips over a hamper full of clothes she needs to put away. Did he say West? Oh, my baby bunnies! Her heart leaps with excitement.

"I'm coming! Tell him to hold on," she yells again, frantically grabbing a comb and trying to put some order to her wet, tangled hair.

"She just got out of the shower, hold on."

Jules blushes and throws the comb down. She doesn't want to look as if she's rushed to fix herself up for him. She hurries across her room, slowing as she rounds the corner to the stairs. Shaking her head, she bounces down the staircase, trying to act cool and collected, especially since she's visible through the window.

"I didn't open it, just like you said," Jason brags the second her bare foot hits the landing of the foyer.

"Thanks, bud."

She lets Jason pull the door open revealing West standing on her front porch with his signature grin. Jason swings open the glass, smiling at him before she has a chance to speak.

"You like *Star Wars?*" he asks incredulously, staring at the vintage tee shirt West is wearing. "I like *Star Wars*, too."

"You do? I still have all of the Lego sets from when I was your age." West smiles and holds the glass door so he can stand there. Her little brother gasps, his eyes growing wide, and she prepares for his inevitable freak out. He's obsessed with *Star Wars* Legos, and can talk about the characters and building sets for hours if you let him.

"I collect them. I have almost all of them. I have this book with all of the sets, and I check them off when I get them. Jules thinks it's silly. She says Legos are *stupid.*"

"What?" she whines and West laughs, his smiling gaze moving from Jason to hers.

"She does, does she?"

"No, she doesn't," she interrupts. She drags Jason from the doorway and shoos him off. "Get out of here."

Jason's excited voice echoes off the walls as he races up the stairs, calling behind him, "I'll go get my Legos!"

She watches him go with a laugh before turning to West with a raised brow. "See what you did? I'll be playing Legos for the rest of the day."

He says 'Sorry' in that 'sorry-not-sorry' way with a smirk to match. "Hi, by the way," he adds, his voice dropping to a more normal tone.

"Hi." She shifts nervously, his proximity making her nerves jumpy. Her hand moves to twist her hair when she remembers it's a wet mess, and she blushes.

"Your brother said you just got out of the shower." He nods toward her wet head. "I should have called first. I can go."

She wants to shout *NO*, but manages to keep her calm. "It's fine. Um, did you want to come in?"

Stepping to the side, she lets West into her foyer, his arm brushing against hers as she pushes the door closed behind him.

"I was driving by and thought maybe we could hang out."

"You were driving by? Where were you heading?" she squints, calling his bluff.

He doesn't bother lying and shrugs instead, before stuffing his hands into his pockets. She's come to recognize this as his nervous gesture.

"Truthfully?"

"The truth is always nice."

West steps closer and allows his scent to swirl around her as he speaks. "You didn't call me back last night," he admits. He removes his hand from his pocket and touches a finger to a bead of water that's worked its way to the tip of her hair. Jules draws a shaky breath as he inches closer. "I wanted to see you. Thought maybe we could go for a ride; get away to a little cornfield I know." His brows rise hopefully.

"I'm on duty today."

"On duty?"

"Yeah." She nods. Jason's voice fills the hallway above and she jumps back. They hear him before they see him. He's happily going on and on about something he's trying to build. "Kid brother duty."

"Oh." He grimaces, lowering his hand and thrusting it back into his pocket. "I really should have called first."

"No, I'm glad you didn't. Er, I mean, I'm glad you're here. You can hang if you don't mind a shadow."

"I'm not a shadow," Jason complains as he bumps into Jules on purpose and holds a spaceship in West's face.

"Oh man, wow. I don't have that one."

"You don't? Want to see my other sets? Can I show him, Jules, please?" he begs.

"Of course, as long as West doesn't mind."

"Do you want to see all my sets? I bet I have a lot you don't, since you're older and don't get them anymore."

"What do you mean I don't get them anymore?" West asks as Jason waves for him to follow upstairs.

Jules follows behind them, happily watching West from behind. His faded jeans fit him to perfection; not too loose to droop, but not too tight either. His blue vintage *Return of the Jedi* tee stretches across his back and molds to each of his muscles. The boy works out…that much is glaringly evident.

She listens as Jason explains how obviously since West is older he doesn't buy Legos anymore, so he can't possibly have all of the new 'cool' sets.

"I'm going to change really quickly, if you don't mind hanging with Jason for a minute."

Her brother continues on to his room and West stops. He flicks his eyes across her body and shakes his head. "You look great. Don't change on my account."

"C'mon West," Jason calls from his room impatiently, making West smile.

"Excuse me, I have some Legos to inspect."

Blushing from West's once-over, Jules enters her room and chooses to stay in the cropped yoga pants and pink workout tee she threw on. No matter how great he says she looks, she needs to take a moment to brush her hair up into a high ponytail and spray on a little body spray. Confident she's presentable, she leaves her room a few minutes later and is surprised by the sounds of a pretend battle coming from her brother's room.

She can make out the mock light saber and blaster sounds. She's watched the movies and played the video games enough to recognize the sounds. Her eyes mist over as she leans against the wall directly outside Jason's room and listens to their playing; West's deep voice blending with her younger brother's higher sounds.

Jason laughs as West makes a strange "Argh" sound and goes silent. His voice begins breathing deeply as he mimics Darth Vader. "You *will* join me," he hisses and Jason giggles; a full-blown, cackling giggle that Jason makes when he's thoroughly amused. Jules can't stand it. She peeks around the door frame to spy on the boys. They're sitting on the floor with little Lego men, pretend fighting.

She fights back tears when her brother looks up, seeing standing there. "Come play, Jules," he invites with a grin.

West looks up too, and what Jules finds makes her heart flip. He doesn't get embarrassed, or drop the guys because he's too cool for playing. Instead he flashes her a smile, picks up another guy and sets him on a ship sitting on the box in front of him.

"How about a snack instead? Why don't you go make some popcorn?" Her voice is thick with emotion and West looks up from his men. His face softening as he searches her face. She imagines he can tell she's emotional. Jason wilts as his eyes go from Jules to West and back.

West notices Jason's concerned face too, and immediately sets him at ease. "Yum! Using the force sure does make me hungry. I could really go for some popcorn." When Jason's face is doubtful, he adds, "Besides, you know we have to follow the Princess's orders, young Padawan."

"She's not a Princess." Jason laughs, but he drops his Lego men and stands anyway.

West also stands and sets his men on the dresser, but his concerned eyes lock on Jules. "I see a Princess."

"Ewww! I'll be downstairs."

Jules laughs at Jason's 'icky' face as he leaves the room. "We'll be right behind you, bud. You can turn on cartoons if you want, or pick a movie," she calls behind him.

She feels West's gaze on her back when she turns and watches Jason walk happily down the hall. A stray tear escapes down her cheek as her brother hums the galactic song. "Thanks for that."

"For what?" he asks, his voice directly behind her.

Her pulse leaps and she throws herself into his chest. "For playing with him. He's had a hard time getting over the tornado, and I haven't seen him truly laugh that way since it happened."

His arms go around her immediately. He rubs the back of her neck, soothing her as his other hand presses against the small of her back.

"Then I'm happy I came by, if only for him."

"You're totally going to lose your bad boy reputation, Rutledge."

"Do I have one?"

"You did, but I'm wondering if it was all part of some elaborate ruse."

"Reputations often are," he offers.

"I'm sorry I didn't call last night. I fell asleep, if you can believe that."

"I thought maybe you changed your mind." Jules hears the nervous hitch in his voice.

"Changed my mind? About what? You and I? Why in the world would you think that?" She pushes up to her toes and presses a kiss on his chin, because that's the only thing she can reach without him leaning down.

"I keep thinking you're going to get your memory back from before the tornado."

"Huh?"

"I know; I'm crazy, right? I don't know if I could handle it, Jules. You're not going to wake up and be all 'Dude, I love Stuart! What am I doing with *this* loser?'"

Jules would laugh if his comment didn't make her so angry. "Dude? What the hell? First, I have all of my memory from before the tornado and I'm not changing my mind. Second, don't call my boyfriend a loser, you loser," she growls, kicking at his foot with hers.

"Your boyfriend, huh?"

"Yeah, my boyfriend. Didn't we agree to this last night? Or are you already leaving me? Is that part of your bad boy charm—love 'em and leave 'em?"

She bites her tongue. All of a sudden he appears to be questioning things, and she mentions the 'L' word. Way to go.

"I told you, gorgeous, I'm not leaving. As for love, well I've never been there with another girl."

"You haven't? Not even with Carley Raine?"

"Nope. Not even Carley. She was fun, but she wasn't love."

Jealousy blooms in her heart and suddenly she kicks herself as she asks the one thing she knows she shouldn't. "And what about me? Am I just fun?"

He presses her against his chest; his hand increasing the pressure on her back, glaring at her almost angrily as he bites out his next words.

"You, Jules Blacklin, are not for fun. You are—" He swallows hard, the muscle in his cheek leaping.

"Never mind, I was playing."

He kisses her, a short peck, which effectively shuts her up before he tells her calmly, "No, you should know. You're not for fun. *You* might even be love." He pauses, stepping back and running a hand over his face. "I think, or at least I'm pretty sure, I could fall in love with you. Does that scare the crap out of you?"

For a few moments she's a fish out of water. She struggles to breathe, much less comprehend what he said and she grabs his face, making him look directly at her.

"The only thing that scares me right now is that I feel the same way."

Pulling his face to hers, she kisses him soundly, but not before she spots the soft warmth in his eyes.

"This is crazy," she whispers against his mouth.

"But real," he counters, his voice as low as hers.

"Perfectly real."

West's hand rounds her hip, curving over her backside much as it did the day before, but this time she doesn't laugh.

"Do I get to see your room?"

She works hard to suppress the knowing smile tugging at her mouth as she pulls him down the hallway into her bedroom. She expects him to attack her the moment they cross the threshold, but instead what she finds when she rounds on him is a serious face as he checks out the room.

Looking around, she quickly scans the floor for anything that might embarrass her. She's always been a neat freak, and today's impromptu visit makes her glad she is. Her room isn't overly girly. There are a few stuffed animals in a chair, and pictures of friends and family cover the two cork boards over the desk that holds her laptop. The white lace curtains covering both windows are about the most feminine items in there. Her bedding is deep gray with white throw pillows, and her bookshelves are covered in books, trophies, framed pictures, and knickknacks she's collected through the years.

West finds the stack of pictures piled on her desk and picks up the one on top. It's the one from the pool party where he's looking at her. She moves to the edge of her bed and waits to hear what he'll say.

"I've never seen these." He holds the picture up and shuffles the others on the desk around. "Man, we look so young."

"We *were* young."

"I would do so many things differently if I could go back to those days," he confesses, and she watches his face fall. "So many things," he whispers.

She's curious what he means and is about to ask for an explanation when Jason yells up the stairs. "Jules! No boys in your room!"

She rolls her eyes as she gets up and stands behind West. He feels far away for a moment, and she touches his back softly, offering some sort of comfort for whatever he's feeling. After a moment, he shakes his head and places the picture back on top of the pile.

"Come on, cheerleader,' he teases quite suddenly; whirling around on her. "No boys allowed in your room."

They ate pizza for dinner and watched the first four *Star Wars* movies with Jason wedged between them. Jason fell asleep against West's side midway through the fourth film and they finished it with West's fingers toying with Jules' hair across the back of the couch. It's close to ten when Jules finally kicks West out. Her parents are due home soon. It's better for West if he doesn't have to face them yet.

They hold hands as she walks him to the door. "I'm not worried about meeting them as your boyfriend, you know. I don't want you to worry about me."

"I know. It's just—I told my mom there was something between us, but—I don't know. I guess I feel like I should tell them we're seeing each other before they walk in on us."

"You're going to tell them though, right?" he asks suspiciously. "I mean, they don't hate me or something, do they?"

"West! Of course not." She pulls him to her lips and presses a quick kiss to his. "They think you're awesome. You saved me, remember?"

Wrapping his arms around her tightly, his mouth slants over hers slowly, coaxing her lips to open to his.

"Shoot, I completely forgot to tell you I'll be gone for the weekend. My dad and I are getting up early and heading to the big game at A&M."

Jules' face falls. "I'm jealous," she admits, rubbing her cheek against his chest. "So I won't see you until Monday?"

"Yeah. My oldest brother, Carson, and his girlfriend, Mindy, live about thirty minutes from campus, so we always stay at their place after the games. Austin lives there too, kinda, and he usually gets to hang too. It's a lot of manly stuff. We probably won't head back until late Sunday. I'll see if I can guilt Dad into coming back earlier so I can stop by."

"No, don't do that. See your brothers and have a good time. I'll be sitting here withering away without you," she teases, although part of her feels the bit of truth in that statement. *Ridiculous.*

"Jules?" She looks up into his face when his soft voice says her name. "Every minute I'm not with you, I'm thinking about you and wanting to be with you."

"Me too," she confesses, kissing him goodbye one last time.

Twenty-Three

The first day of her senior year rolls around the following Monday; two weeks late and in defiance of all the wishes and prayers from Jules that this year would never happen. Unbeknownst to anyone, she cries silently in the shower for a good twenty minutes before she's able to pull herself together. Makeup covers the dark circles and blush makes her pale skin glow, but inside? Inside she is numb.

The night before, she has another dream with Tanya in it. They're running hand in hand, laughing and shouting the way they did on Friday nights, when they ran across the football field. The crowd cheers, florescent lights shine down and they are happy. A piercing scream from Tanya's chest replaces the laughter on their lips as a giant black cloud falls from the sky and lands in front of them. The powerful funnel tears at Tanya and her hand is ripped violently from Jules' grasp as she disappears. Before Jules can scream, she's hit in the back by something heavy, which jolts her awake with a cry. The nightmare leaves her shaken, yet again.

As she puts the finishing touches on her first day look, her cell buzzes on her nightstand.

Spike: Hey gorgeous! Sure I can't pick you up?

He asked the same question several times over the weekend. Her parents are totally against her riding on his bike, and his car is currently with his older brother at school while his is in the shop. Katie and Jules are going to ride together; the way they would have if Tanya were alive.

Jules: You know I'm riding with Katie

West: I know, but I can't wait to see your face. I want everyone at Rossview to know you're mine. Sit in the car & wait for me?
Jules: LOL. You're kidding, right?
West: No
Jules: West!
West: You don't know those guys. They're vultures when a hot girl is around. You're wearing a bag, right?

She laughs as she looks down at her short dress and ankle boots. Replying 'Of course. See you soon!' she is happy to feel a smidge lighter as she makes her way down the stairs.

It's too early for Jason to be awake yet, but Jules is surprised to find her mom and dad in the kitchen, sitting over coffee.

"Good morning, my senior girl!" her mom sings; awfully bright and cheery for such an early hour.

Jules mimics the caveman 'Ugh' and grabs a glass for juice.

"Do you have time to eat something? I made bacon. Want me to fry up an egg?"

Jules hasn't eaten a 'real' breakfast before school since elementary school. In middle school it transitioned to Pop-tarts and Toaster Strudels. She converted to Slim Fast shakes for a while in the erroneous assumption that her tiny frame was too athletic, thanks to years of gymnastics and cheerleading. By her sophomore year, she became more secure with herself and reverted back to a quick Pop-tart out the door, which is undoubtedly the breakfast of champions. Starbucks is also a morning staple, especially when she chose to ride with the girls over Stuart.

With a quick glance at her watch, she pops the microwave open and snags a strip of extra crispy bacon.

"Katie will be here any minute. We didn't know how long it would take us to get there with all the detours and traffic." She sets her empty cup on the counter and grabs a water bottle and the lunch she packed the night before.

"Picture first."

"Mom, I need to run," Jules lies. She isn't in the mood to commemorate this day.

"Oh, just a quick one," her mom insists, already waving the camera in her hand. With a sigh, Jules trudges to the front door where she always poses for the annual picture. "Say 'senior'!" her mom sings teasingly as the flash blinds Jules.

"Yay," Jules grumbles. Her dad frowns while her mom's face sinks.

"It's not much to ask for, Jules. One smile. It's your last first day of school, honey," he reminds her softly.

"I suppose I should be dancing, seeing as how I'm so lucky to be alive," Jules snaps.

"Honey?"

Katie's red car pulls up in front of the house and Jules fakes a smile. "Have a good day."

With a quick jerk of the door, she stalks to the car without another word to her parents. How can they be so insensitive to how she feels today? A first day of school picture? What did it matter anymore?

She folds herself into Katie's little coupe and Katie speaks the exact thoughts she has. "Too soon to skip?"

"Probably."

"Bummer."

They pull away from the curb, her parents standing in the door watching them, and Jules sighs heavily for the one-hundredth time that morning.

Katie eyes her carefully as she speeds through the streets of her neighborhood. "So, I've been a mess all morning. You?"

"Yeah. It wasn't supposed to be like this, K."

"I know," she agrees sadly. Jules turns to Katie and smiles slightly at her outfit. They'd all gone shopping for school clothes together a few weeks ago, planning their matching—yet slightly different—back-to-school outfits. They'd done it for years, in honor of their matching backpacks on their first day of Kindergarten when they all met. Today it consists of matching dresses and boots, but the dresses are each different color schemes. They're a trendy Aztec print, but where hers is earth-toned orange and turquoise, Katie's is pastel-toned pink and blue. Tanya would have worn brighter, almost fluorescent tones.

It's reminiscent of their personalities. Jules, the laid-back, earthier girl; Katie, the sweet one; and Tanya, the loud, boisterous one. Jules sniffs barely containing the pain that comes with the memories.

"We have just enough time."

"For?"

"Tradition, Juju. Tradition."

They pull into the Starbucks drive-thru along with the hordes of other patrons and Jules brightens. Maybe a frappe will get her day going. Candy Crenshaw and two other girls from Hillsdale walk out of the Starbucks and Katie waves.

"Jules! Katie!" Candy shrieks and bounces to the car.

"Whoa, she must have ordered a double," Jules mumbles to Katie.

"Y'all are heading to Rossview, aren't you?" Candy pouts. Jules thinks it a little disingenuous. Man, when did she become so jaded with her friends? Candy has always been an annoyingly peppy attention seeker, but they never had an issue with one another.

"How are you doing, Jules?" Candy asks, and Jules snaps from her thoughts.

"Huh?"

"I was saying I heard about you and Stuart. How are you? I can't believe the golden couple is no more. Everything is going to be so different this year."

"You think?" she mocks Candy's high-pitched voice, throwing in a fake laugh. Katie glares at her reproachfully, so Jules rolls her eyes and offers up a more politically correct answer. "I'm good, thanks Candy. It was a mutual breakup and we're both moving on."

"That's not what I heard. I heard Stuart is devastated, although I'm sure those Houston girls will comfort him when he's ready."

The car behind them honks once and Candy steps back from the window when Katie points out that it's time for them to move forward in line.

"Well girls, technically we're supposed to be enemies now, but let's hang soon, 'kay?" The three of them wave gaily and rush away.

"For the love of all things holy, *please* run her over," Jules mutters as they walk in front of Katie's car; their little skirts flapping with the breeze.

"Jeez, Jules. When did you become so angry?"

"*Me?* Did you hear her?"

"It's Candy. You know she doesn't have a brain. We ignore her rambling, remember?"

Static filters through the car window and Katie orders three Grande mocha frappes with extra espresso.

"Three?"

Katie finally looks much like Jules feels. Her voice cracking slightly as she repeats "Tradition". They're silent as they pay and wait for their drinks.

"Hey, Candy said Stuart is devastated by our break-up, didn't she? Where would she hear a thing like that?"

"Come on, Jules. Don't bother thinking about it. You know gossip and Candy."

She eyes her friend skeptically but lets it go. A few other teens from Hillsdale come and go as they sit idling. Who's going to Rossview with them and who was sent to Robinson or the other two schools nearby?

"All right, so maybe I planned this a little too much," Katie admits once they get their drinks and right before they pull out of the

Starbucks parking lot. She grabs her iPhone and fumbles with the screen to pull up her music. As if they share a mind, Jules feels a conflicted smile coming on. The speakers go live with the acapella version of 'Don't Stop Believing' and she breaks out into laughter. This has been their song—hers, Katie's, and Tanya's—for years, since the first episode of *Glee*. What a fitting song to play today.

"I'm so glad you thought of this!" Jules shouts over the singing.

"One more stop." She grins back at her and Jules knows where they're headed. A quick glance at the clock shows they should have barely enough time, but Jules doesn't care—she'll be late for today.

A few minutes later they pull into the memorial gardens where Tanya is buried. The winding road through the property is covered in huge shade trees, and flowers bloom along the way as they make it to the back of the property where the pond and Tanya's final resting place are located.

Jules gasps when they drive over a small ridge and she spots several cars she recognizes parked along the road in front of her.

"K!" she cries, tears springing to her eyes immediately. Katie slows to a stop at the curb behind Jeff's car and puts the vehicle in park.

"I couldn't start this day without her, Jules, and I was kinda banking on you feeling the same way." She twists in her seat, a stray tear running down her cheek under her sunglasses.

"I totally feel the same. Of course I do."

Grabbing the extra frappe, they climb out of the car. Katie waits for Jules to reach her side and they thread their arms together and walk toward the grave site.

"Can we try to hold it together, though? I don't want to start our first day at Ross resembling a raccoon," Jules teases. Katie flips her glasses up and reveals make-up free eyes with a wink. "You skank! You could have warned me we'd be doing this."

"Sorry. I brought my make-up though, so no worries."

Smiling and crying at the same time—that is something she never knew she could do until Tanya's death. She's laughed so hard at cheesy movies that she's cried, but to cry because her heart and soul are devastated and yet be able to laugh too? Nope—that's a first. Tommy's truck is parked in front of Jeff's car and Jules smiles; happy they're here for this too. She's thinking about how much Tanya would love this attention as she passes Tommy's truck and there, sitting at the curb hidden by Tommy's monster truck, she spots a black motorbike and freezes.

"A little birdie may have told me," Katie hints, and the last of Jules' walls break down. She hurries toward the grave site, dragging Katie along since their arms are linked together. West is here, *for her!* Her whole body feels warm as the tears start to drip from her eyes. Her artfully applied mascara and eyeliner burn her eyes.

They walk around a large copse of trees and bushes, and there the girls find Jeff, Tommy, and West standing before them. Tommy's kneeling at the grave with his head low as if he's talking to Tanya, and Katie lets out a choked sob when she sees him. Jeff and West stand back next to a tree; respectfully giving Tommy some privacy. Jules' eyes lock on West and she notices the way he leans casually against the tree with his feet crossed at the ankles. In his hand he holds a single rose.

Jeff turns toward Tommy, his low voice whispering something before he turns toward her and Katie. Tommy stands and wipes his arm across his face before he turns to face them as well.

Jules carries the extra frappe in her hand, but it doesn't stop her from walking straight to West and throwing her arms around him. They don't speak, neither of them, they simply hug. He wraps one arm tightly around her back, and the other takes its place at the base of her skull. She feels his chin resting on the top of her head, and through all the pain she feels, she also feels relief. West brings strength and relief with him every time he touches her.

"This isn't a bag you're wearing," he whispers, and she lets out a half-laugh, half-sob. Her chest hurts from holding it all in. "You look gorgeous, though."

His lips press onto the top of her head and she tilts up so he can place another kiss on her forehead.

"I can't believe you're here."

West releases her head and wipes the tears from her cheek using his thumb. "I care about you, why wouldn't I be here?"

"You were playing with me this morning?" she asks, thinking about his text earlier asking to pick her up.

"Was I?" he teases, his bad boy smile locked firmly in place. "My bad. Actually, had you told me you wanted me, I would have come."

Slowly she stretches up and kisses his lips. "I did want you, but I knew Katie would need me today as much as I needed her."

"I missed you this weekend. Next home game you're coming with us."

"Deal."

He smiles at her with that sexy smile that could stop time. She has something more important to do today though, so she pulls away reluctantly and turns toward the others. Katie stands encircled in Jeff's arms, waiting on her with her eyes fixed on the grave. The headstone hasn't come in yet, but There's a plaque and piles of flowers covering the fresh, grassy mound.

Holding hands, they place the frappe amongst the flowers and stand back in silence.

"It's not going to be the same without you, Ya-ya," Jules whispers.

"You'd be proud, though. Juju's already picking up your bitchiness. What'd you do? Possess her?" Katie quips with a watery smile at Jules.

"Help us all now," Tommy mutters and the five of them laugh lightly.

This is it. Life after the storm, life without their third musketeer. It will be different for sure, but as she stares at West's hand tightly clasping hers, she feels a peace come over her. Peace, and a spark of courage telling her she can make it.

"To senior year and to Tanya," Katie toasts, holding up her frappe. Jules taps it with her own and they all chime in. "To Tanya."

Epilogue

"That morning, standing there toasting Tanya, was a profound one. The first day of school suddenly made things crystal clear to me. Life as we knew it was gone. We didn't speak much as we walked to our cars and loaded up to head for Rossview. New year, new school, new reality," Jules huffs, almost disdainful of the story. "Yeah, life as we knew it was gone."

Pulling a tissue from the box on the floor by her feet, Jules wipes the tears away at the memories. She checks the clock on the wall and is surprised at how long she's been telling her story. She stands and stretches her aching limbs. Taking a sip of her tea, she talks randomly at the camera, though she knows it will be edited out.

"It's funny how, now that I'm at this part of the story, I'm finding it harder to tell."

She paces the floor a few times; her right hand rubbing over her left. She used to have a habit of twirling the band she wore on her ring finger. The ring is no longer there, but the habit is hard to break.

"Sorry, I guess I could have paused this," she speaks to the nameless faces who will edit the video into a pretty package for their film project. She sighs. "All right, let me finish."

Settling back in her chair, she tucks both legs under her this time as she begins again . . .

"If you've seen one high school, you would think you've pretty much seen them all, right? Rossview is pretty comparable to Hillsdale. A typical-looking Texas school; two story building with a sprawling campus that looks eerily similar to a jail on the outside. Inside, though? Well *that's* a whole other ball game."

"Guilt. A painful, lonely feeling. It seeps into your pores slowly as you go through life day by day. Like a disease, it blackens your heart with thoughts and memories of what you did, or in my case, what you didn't do."

Surviving the storm was only the beginning for Jules. Surviving the guilt? That is something only love can help her overcome.

Out of Ruins

From The Wreckage, book 2

Available NOW

Want to read **From The Wreckage** from West's POV?
Check out **WEST**.
Available NOW

WEST: A From The Wreckage Novel

One

"Still can't miss a game?" Jeff jumps onto the bench of the picnic table at The Ice Shack and takes a seat next to me. I've been sitting here watching students from Hillsdale High show up in droves for the past twenty minutes. The Shack is always the place to hang after Friday night games; with tonight being the first game of the new school year, it's especially packed.

His shoulder knocks into mine. "Why do you keep showing up if it bothers you?"

"Who said it bothers me?"

"Seriously?" Jeff's right brow cocks up as one corner of his mouth turns down.

"Whatever," I mutter. He knows me well. I kick at his foot with the toe of my boot, changing the subject as we watch the crowd. "You played a good game tonight. A little weak to the right, but you keep it up and A&M won't regret recruiting you." He plays defensive back for our high school and he's exceptional. It's why he's been heavily recruited by every school in the state—and then some.

He shakes off my comment. "It's a long season, West." He sighs, "Wow, this is it. Senior year."

"Senior year," I repeat, sending a knowing smile his way. "Hard to believe we've almost made it."

Jeff scoffs. "Hell, it's hard to believe we've survived this long. Hey, why don't you come hang out with the living for a change tonight?" He nods his blond head toward the crowd of jocks and other students from Hillsdale congregating around the parking lot. I shrug, ignoring his intentional dig at my choice of friends, and am spared the need to refuse by the uptick in crowd noise that grabs Jeff's attention.

A smile forms on his face and he rubs his hands together before hopping down from the table. He walks backwards, motioning over his shoulder to the car sitting in the middle of the parking lot, the headlights flickering on and off. "Gotta run. My girl's here."

"You and Katie? Again, man?" I groan, although I know it's pointless to argue. "Will you ever learn?" I call after him as I survey the scene behind his back. The car belongs to Tanya Rivera—Katie's best friend—and she's unable to move thanks to two guys who are re-enacting their own version of Magic Mike in the beam of her headlights. Cheers at their antics ring out.

"Come over," Jeff offers again, and I shake my head at him and the showboaters. "Don't pretend those little skirts have no effect on you, Rutledge. I know where, and who, your eyes focus on," Jeff shouts with laughter as he jogs backward to join the others. I flip him off before turning my back to the crowd.

Instead of joining them I remain seated on the table to the left of The Shack, gazing at the shadowy field before me. The late August air is humid and a trail of sweat trickles down the small of my back as a light breeze picks up. It's the last weekend of summer break. Come Monday, I'm a senior; I'm not sure if I'm relieved or not. I have no concrete plans for my life after high school.

Not anymore.

I'll still go to A&M—because it's what Rutledge boys do—but I won't be doing what I'd always planned. Instead I'll spend my Saturdays cheering on one of my best friends, Jeff, and my brother Austin as they chase their dreams on the football field without me. The notion leaves a bitter taste in my mouth. A hollow sensation sinks into my chest, but I push it aside as my ears pick up the cheers and name calling around me.

The loud blare of a horn puts a smile on my face as Tanya's curses carry from the parking lot to my hiding spot. Funny enough, I don't feel as though I'm missing out on much. I enjoy it here in my dark corner away from the people I've known for most of my life. Flipping a flask around between my fingers, I contemplate what Jeff said when he first showed up. Going to football games, the ones I should be playing in, doesn't bother me. Not usually. It's been four years since I took an official snap, threw a pass under the Friday night lights, and hoisted a teammate into the air after an amazing connection. Four years since I gave it up. Yet I show up to every game my old teammates play and I watch. I find myself studying their moves and deciphering the playbook mentally. I curse their stupid mistakes as though they affect me, and I begrudgingly cheer their wins.

Begrudgingly.

My breath catches at the word. Perhaps I care more than I'd like to admit, but it's too late now.

"Poor Tanya, that can't be comfortable."

The unmistakable voice of Jules Blacklin—head cheerleader, town sweetheart, and the Quarterback's girlfriend—interrupts my complicated thoughts. Startled, I shift and look over my shoulder. Jules has taken a seat at my picnic table with her back to me. Her tiny cheerleading uniform hugs her figure; the pleated skirt riding low on her hips offers me a tantalizing glance at the smooth skin of her lower back. I bite back an admiring smile and a dozen dirty thoughts. "You always talk to yourself, cheerleader?"

Red hair flies around as Jules' head snaps my way. This girl is gorgeous, as one would expect a cliché golden girl in high school to be. She looks at me, her blue eyes wide with surprise; she obviously didn't see me sitting here in the dark. I suppress my grin as I study the little wrinkles in her forehead and the pink tint to her face. Even in the dark her skin reminds me of a damn peach. I recall a time, years ago, when I touched those smooth cheeks and gazed into those crystal blues. The thought stirs something within. *Damn it*. While I sit here and lose my ever-loving mind at the sight of her, she merely blinks as though she's trying to recognize me. I attempt to not let her indifference bruise my ego.

"Excuse me?"

"You're excused, Buffy," I drawl. I grin at my clever joke as I tip my head to the side and allow my eyes to rove over her backside again. We go way back—elementary school, pee wee football, middle school team events—she's part of a past life. I've spoken to Jules a handful of times in the past four years. Less since she started dating Stuart Daniels during our sophomore year. I've watched her though; she's hard to ignore.

Jules studies me, her head tilting side to side before one russet brow arches and a self-satisfied look washes over her face. "Does that make you Spike? Sitting here brooding in the dark with your flask?"

I don't suppress my approval of her witty comeback. *Touché*. I lift the flask in question, saluting her with a mock toast. Jules' eyes narrow on my mouth and a million thoughts whirl through my mind. Why the hell is she sitting here? I assumed she'd walk away the moment I spoke, and I certainly didn't expect her to fire teasing comments back at me. But now, not only has she remained sitting, but she's watching me. No, not watching me, she's watching my mouth as though she wants to taste the liquid dripping from my bottom lip. My stomach clenches at the thought and I swallow hard. Making the decision to enjoy this rare encounter, I face her fully and lean my forearms on my knees. As though the weight of my stare is too much, Jules stands with a shake of her head.

"I think I could live with you calling me Spike," I say, hoping for another round of verbal boxing with her. A breeze rolls by, lifting her red and white pleated skirt. A guy's gotta love those little skirts.

"Really?" Her hand presses her pleats down. "You do know Buffy and Spike hated each other?" she asks. There's surprise in her tone. She sounds hurt somehow, and I can't fathom why she'd feel disappointment. I brush the ridiculous notion aside.

The lights inside The Shack flicker once, but I pay little attention. I'm too engaged in verbal sword play with a beautiful girl. Jules pointed out Buffy and Spike's disdain for one another, but I'm reminded of the enemies-to-lovers story arc between the characters. Silently thanking my ex Carley for forcing her addiction to the show upon me when we were dating, I lower my voice and correct Jules' statement with a grin.

"At first."

Her eyes narrow. "At first?"

"Jules," interrupts Katie as she jogs our way. "Can you believe this? Every freaking weekend they do this crap. Can't we just get Tanya and go? I'm so tired of all the pissing contests."

Straightening, I pay Jeff's on-again, off-again girl no heed as my eyes lock on Jules' eyes. I will her to grasp the meaning behind my comment. Katie barely glances my way as she grabs Jules' hand, ready to pull her back to her friends, but Jules doesn't budge. I sense the moment she catches it, the double meaning of my words.

Her blue eyes widen and she stammers, "Oh, at first."

Her face lights up and I'm transfixed. Without warning, my memories fly back to the seventh grade and a kiss with the girl I wanted to impress so badly that I manufactured our being picked for the age old game of Seven Minutes in Heaven. This is the girl Jeff was referring to only moments ago as he laughed at me. The one my eyes always go to, the one who might have been mine once upon a time, if not for cancer.

If not for Stuart Daniels.

If not for my being a quitter.

Jules Blacklin.

My memories mean nothing as the lights flicker on and off once more and beside me Katie whines as she tugs on Jules' arm. "Come on."

Irritated at my thoughts, I salute the girls with a chuckle. "See ya around, Buff," I say as I slide down from the picnic table, forcing myself to leave.

Or I would have left if not for the shouting.

Katie's angry interruption makes sense now as I look to where she came from. A fight has broken out in the parking lot and I shake my head, mumbling beneath my breath, "Stupid pricks."

I'm not able to identify the participants rolling around on the ground before their shouts are drowned out by a sound infinitely more terrifying.

My pulse quickens as the piercing scream of the early warning storm sirens go off, making me and everyone around jump at the signal. The Ice Shack goes silent and I hold my breath as I look past the crowd and down the highway toward the normally cheerful town of Tyler, Texas. It currently resembles a disco, the lights flashing on and off, and I know—we all know—something isn't right.

PAPER PLANES
and other things we lost

Mindy Hayes &
Michele G. Miller

PROLOGUE

Dear Amber,

Did you know you're more likely to be attacked by a shark than die in a plane crash? I find that interesting since I never go in the ocean, but I've been on a plane ten times. So, I guess I'm more likely to die in a plane crash than be attacked by a shark, but maybe it's different for you.

I thought beginning this letter as if you already know me would make the concept of a total stranger writing to you a little less weird, but now that I've thought about it, I realize my fascination with plane crash facts might be weirder. But I like weird. So, hi. If you didn't catch it from my return address, I'm Ruby Kaminski from Fremonton, California.

My mom died on Flight 397 with your parents. Though, can we really say they died when we have no idea what actually happened to them? Let's refer to them as MIA. No, I'm not in denial. I'm painfully aware that they aren't coming back, but I like facts. And the truth of the matter is most of the people on Flight 397 are MIA.

You're probably wondering how I managed to get your address. I have my ways. Besides, I thought it might be good to connect with someone who understands what I'm going through. Though I believe our circumstances are entirely different, and there's no way for me to understand what you're going through, I'm hoping we can relate to one another on some level.

Do you ever wonder if, after the plane exploded, the passengers were washed up onto a remote island, and now they are kicking back, drinking coconut milk and sun tanning under a palm tree? Maybe they are eating fresh seafood cooked over a fire and sleeping under the stars?

It's a nice thought, don't you think?

If you're okay with weird, feel free to write me back. I'm full of it.

Sincerely,

Ruby Kaminski

JUST ANOTHER DAY

FRIDAY, JANUARY 1

"Happy New Year!"

"Screw you."

Screw. You. Those are my first words of the new year? Ha! Bet this is going to be a stellar year.

"Awe, give me a kiss." The shrill voice shouts the slurred words in my ear. I may be deaf now, thank you very much. Bright pink cable knit sleeves drape around my neck, the wearer's dark blonde mop of hair assaulting me. She isn't at all familiar. What the heck, man? I pluck her wrists from my shoulders and she falls away. Freedom! I make my escape.

A heavy beat ricochets off the wall as I work my way upstairs. I stop midway and glance over the banister. There's a sea of bodies occupying the dim room below. Revelry is everywhere. It's 1993—a new year. The year of graduation, the year we start college, the year we become adults. A circle of girls bursts into laughter directly below me, one of them blowing a noise maker, as their hips move to the rhythm pulsating from the speakers. I should be down there, too. They're celebrating the beginning of a new year. I'm celebrating the end of the old one.

I turn my back to the revelers. Closing my eyes, I press my knuckles between them and rub the skin in circles. Between the obnoxiously loud music, cheerful party goers, and asthma-inducing cigarette smoke, I've developed a headache in the three minutes I've been here. Why does she do this to herself?

Man, these parties suck. The smoking and drinking, the random hook-ups sessions and fights . . . and the crap like this—the random body before me. The poor guy is propped against the wall, passed out between two steps. I carefully step over him. How far would he roll if I shoved his shoulder? Humpty Dumpty sat on a wall, Humpty Dumpty had a great fall. Wow. My foul mood is her fault.

I move forward, side-stepping a couple near the top of the stairs, and scan the hallway. She's nowhere to be found. On to knocking on doors it is. Man, this knight in shining armor routine is old. I'm sick of coming to her rescue, but here I am doing it again.

Slamming my fist on each door, I jiggle the handles and call out her name.

"Amber?" The first door glides open, revealing a room full of teens sitting in a cloud of smoke staring back at me. No Amber.

Door two is locked. No answer. I pound harder. "Amber?"

"She's not in here," a vaguely familiar voice replies. How many doors have I knocked on looking for my sister in the past six months? Too many if people recognize us.

The door at the end of the long hallway opens, the party host himself walking out. Dude's dressed for July at the beach, not January in Pennsylvania, with his open button-up shirt and low hanging shorts. What an idiot.

"George, where's Amber?"

"Hey, man." George lifts his hand for a high five. "Happy New . . ." His salutation cuts off as I stalk forward. I hurry his way before he can think to close the bedroom door. I should have saved my breath; he doesn't bother with discretion. The prick.

He stumbles, his bloodshot eyes blinking rapidly as his back hits the wall. I crowd his personal space, rejecting his high five and pressing my palm into his chest. The potent stench of alcohol and sweat rolling off him could singe nose hairs. "You've got to be kidding me." If she's in this room . . . I compose myself and shove open the door.

My eyes leave George's face and he inches away. Forget him, Brett, he's not worth the swollen knuckles.

There she is.

Okay, maybe he is worth the hassle. My jaw clenches.

Amber's perched on the edge of a disheveled king-size bed. Her face is blank as she slips her shirt over her head. I inhale deeply, averting my gaze and locking the door behind me. Ruffled pillows, floral paintings, and a feminine wallpaper border decorate the room. This is his parents room? Sick.

"No lectures."

"Psh, why would I bother wasting my words on one of those?"

"Brett." Her eyes and her tone hold a plea. I've heard it before. Remain calm. "I'm bringing you home."

I should take hold of her skinny shoulders and shake her like a rag doll until she learns some sense, but the method wouldn't work on her. Nothing works with her. I'm prepared to tell her as much when her tears begin.

"Did he—" How do I ask the question? Did he hurt you? Force you? Why is she crying?

"Hmmm?" She swipes her knuckles across her damp cheek. "Did he what?" She gapes at me. "Oh! No. B, I'm fine. He . . ." Her words tangle together and she stops trying. I roll my eyes. It's hard to find the energy for anything more.

Walking into the adjoining bathroom, Amber flips on the light and straightens herself. She wipes at the black streaks below her eyes, a tissue pressed against her lips as her fingers comb her hair into something presentable. It's as though I'm watching a scene from a movie. One I've seen many, many times. I recognize these movements for what they are; she's putting herself back together again. Humpty Dumpty's tune echoes in my mind again. When will rescuing her stop working? At what point will she no longer be able to put herself back together again?

Her hands press palm down on the vanity as she leans forward. She stands there, her nose pressing against the mirror, studying her reflection for two whole minutes before she straightens, shakes her head, and flips off the light.

We leave the house in silence.

She slips into the passenger seat of my car and buckles up. "How was your date?"

How typical of her, ignoring what she's done and speaking to me as though it's merely another mundane day. I close my eyes, gripping the steering wheel.

Calm down, Brett.

She's struggling.

She's hurting.

I need to help her figure things out, but, man, I want to run away from this—from her—and everything I've taken on over the past six months.

Amber coughs, rubbing her hands together, blatantly reminding me of the below freezing temperatures and the fact that we're sitting in an ice box. I crank the engine and the heater kicks on.

"My date was great," I shift into drive. "Right up until the moment I had to leave and rescue my idiot sister."

Her sharp inhale is like a sneeze in a library. Recognition dawns on her face. A wry smile crosses her lips as my angry one challenges her. "You're right." Her head cocks to the left, her brow lifting. "I *am* an idiot," she concedes.

Before June, I would have laughed and gloated at her easy concession. Not tonight though. Tonight, I don't want to be right. I don't want to see my sister in this light. I simply want her to stop what she's doing.

Yep, happy New Year to me.

PAPER PLANES and Other Things We Lost
Available Everywhere NOW

a note from the author . . .

Thank you so much for picking up *From The Wreckage*. First, I want to say that while there IS a real Tyler, Texas, this story features my own version of Tyler. In other words, it's totally made up and anything resembling any person, place or thing is purely coincidental.

Second, if you enjoyed Jules and West's story, I'd love for you to take a moment and write a quick review on the site where you purchased the book. It's super easy and helps me out a bunch since I'm an Indie author, and we need all the help we can get. Also, share! Word of mouth is our biggest marketing tool so please tell your friends to check *From The Wreckage* out. I appreciate it beyond belief.

I love hearing from readers so feel free to chat me up on Twitter or Facebook.

Most importantly, keep reading! I hope you'll check out some of my other titles, but also those of other Indie authors. There are a ton of amazing stories out there waiting to be discovered by you!

Acknowledgments

Each time I finish a novel I feel as though I could write another, simply to thank all of those who keep me ticking every day. I could never thank everyone who touches me, in one way or another, on a daily basis. I can't even begin to try. BUT, I shall...

To everyone who buys, reads, and reviews my books—thank you. Plain and simple. I'm especially touched by those who take the time to send me notes on Facebook. I can't tell you how I feel when I see a new note telling me what you think of a character or a new review talking about the storyline. A million thanks to each of you.

My super fans and street team—Chele's Belles—these ladies give me advice when I'm stuck, they BETA for me, they check out the teasers I create and help pimp me out. For that I am forever grateful: Cheri Gracey, Samantha Eaton-Roberts, Kayla Hargaden, Danielle Young, Tanya Johnson, Megan Bagley, Jessica Smith, Chelcie Holguin, Mandy Anderson, Marla Wenger, Destiny Love, Megan Toffoli, Nancy Byers, Ali Hymer, Laura Helseth and Tess Watson

My #Fierce5 sisters, Christy Foster, Mindy Hayes, Starla Huchton and Sarah Ashley Jones—words are not necessary. You girls complete me.

Honorable mention to the fabulous Tess Watson who has been beside me since day one. You're a #F5 sidekick *wink*.

My SUPER Alpha gal, Megan Toffoli—I can't do half of what I do without you. Why? Because you keep me sane, you make me laugh, you let me bug you all day long and you read the junk I write and tell me it's junk. Then you read the good stuff and you praise it. Thank you!

Super Alpha gal #2, Jessica Smith—you have been a blessing too. Xander appreciates all the advocating you do on his behalf and I appreciate all the fangirling excitement you bring to the crazy things I show you.

Playlist

Music is a huge part of every book I write. Below is a list of some of the songs that were played during the writing of From The Wreckage...

Delta Rae – Chasing Twisters
City and Colour – Little Hell
Throw The Fight – I Just Died In Your Arms
Elisa – Hallelujah
Sarah McLachlan – I Will Remember You—Live
Seether – Broken
Elisa – Dancing
Phil Collins – You'll Be In My Heart (Phil Version)
Paolo Nutini – Autumn
P!nk – The Great Escape
Green River Ordinance – Dark Night
Amber Pacific – Forever
Luke Bryan – Drink A Beer
Gavin DeGraw – Everything Will Change
Tyrone Wells – Use Somebody (Bonus Track)
Green River Ordinance – Resting Hour
Glee Cast – Don't Stop Believin'
Train – This Ain't Goodbye
Ron Pope – Good Day

This is a partial list. To find the rest of the amazing songs I listen to you can check me out on Spotify

About The Author

Michele writes novels with fairy tale love for everyday life. Romance is always central to her plots where the genres range from Coming of Age Fantasy and Drama to New Adult Romantic Suspense.

Sign up for my monthly newsletter (http://bit.ly/MGMNews) to keep up with all the latest, exclusive first peeks and other perks.

Email: authormichelegmiller@gmail.com
Facebook: https://www.facebook.com/AuthorMicheleGMiller
Twitter: @chelemybelles
Instagram: Chelemybelles
Website: www.michelegmillerbooks.com

Made in the USA
Lexington, KY
13 October 2016